The Ghost

of

Homer Lusta

Bob Taylor

Cover design by Anthony Taylor

Author invites comments: roarta@hotmail.com
Author website: www.BobWritesForYou.com

Printed in the United States of America.

ISBN: 978-1-4907-2047-0 (sc)
ISBN: 978-1-4907-2046-3 (hc)
ISBN: 978-1-4907-2048-7 (e)

Library of Congress Control Number: 2013921934

Trafford rev. 11/27/2013

 www.trafford.com
North America & international
toll-free: 1 888 232 4444 (USA & Canada)
fax: 812 355 4082

Other Books by Bob Taylor

So Sweet Justice
Love Lost, Found Anew, in a Cruel Asian War
Kindle Books

Operation Hannibal
Never Abandon a Fallen Comrade
Kindle Books

A Few Good Memories
Tales from Marine Corps Boot Camp
Trafford Books

Contents

Prologue

"Dark Clouds Risin'"

©Carole Johnson

My name is Homer Lusta. Jus' call me Homer. Least thass what it usta be when I was livin' down on Earth. But I ain't there no more. When I left, God seen fit to give me a new home up on High. Blest Pete, if you ain't never been up on High, you wudn't b'lieve jus' how good a final restin' place it is.

Wadn't long ago I met me this new friend. I been goin' 'round a long time, lookin' for jus' the right person to help me. I run into a lot of people, but the first sight o' this new friend o' mine, I knowed he was the one.

How I found 'im was, I was lurkin' 'bout in a little town in Georgia when I seen him settin' peaceful-like on his back porch, holdin' a little glass in his hand. He kep' sippin' outta that glass and steady lookin' at a round black ball thing settin' on top o' three skinny legs. Whole thing was 'bout three foot high. Look like he was cookin' his supper 'cause it smelt real good and smoke was pourin' out. It didn't make no sense why he was cookin' his supper outside the house. His house was right decent lookin' and I figure he oughta be 'ffordin' of a inside stove.

You see, my story 'bout my war been wellin' up inside o' me for a long time and I got a hankerin' to tell it. It begin in 1861 when I wadn't but twenty-two and this country done got in a peck o' trouble. We git drawed in a real bad war. Ever'body 'round home was mad 'bout how them dad blasted Yankees was comin' down and messin' with us. Ain't that jus' like Yankees? Bunch o' boys from home begin joinin' the army to help git things set straight. So I figure I oughta join up too and help out. Well, guess you know that war never turned out too good for our side. Some things was good for me. Some things was bad. I won't talk no more 'bout that right now 'cause itta git told later.

Them years after that war, I set back restin' 'mongst the joys God got salted 'way in Heaven. I begin givin' a heap o' thought to what all's been wrote 'bout my Rebel boys. It ain't been real good. Then, Blest Pete, when some fine boy do speak kindly words, it don't last long 'cause busybodies git down on what he say. So I set my mind to fix it. I 'cided to find me a nice boy I could tell 'way it actual was and maybe he kin write stuff oughta be said.

I begin goin' to diff'rent places 'round the South, keepin' myself a apparition, a ghost, or one o' them things plain folks can't see, and lookin' for the right boy. After all my lookin', Blest Pete, I seen this boy cookin' on his porch and I knowed he the bes' one. So, one day I turn myself visible and set on his porch, right down side of 'im in a chair. I think it scared 'im half to death, so I said real quick, "It's OK. I'm jus' Homer Lusta and I wanna be your friend."

He final calm down and soon we git busy bein' friends. He say his name was Bob and he usual write his own books, all by hisself. Well, I told him what I was aimin' at and first thing he said was he ain't got a heap o' time to waste. I begin talkin' praiseworthy stuff 'bout that war and he listen more and more. Wadn't long 'fore he said it was gettin' late and he better git the food in the house or his wife gonna git raucous mad. I figure I done lost out, but then he said if I was still a mind to, come back the next day in the afternoon, so we kin talk secret. He say he don't want no neighbors thinkin' he a nut.

So, the next day me and my new friend, Old Bob, thass what I call him now, right to his face, set down and jaw a whole heap. He made me 'gree to buckle hard down and tell truthful stuff. I 'gree I was gonna tell him good things and bad things, nuthin' but gospel truth, so he kin write it down. Old Bob say that was good but I gotta recollect real hard 'cause lotta people livin' now ain't certain 'bout the real truth o' that war and they might be please to learn somethin'.

Old Bob say to first talk 'bout the Lustas. Main thing I told 'im, they was five of us. Max was our Pa. Ma's name was Minnie and she drop me in 1839. Lotta come two year after that. Last one out was little brother, Lack, in 1847.

Pa work our little farm outside Dodgetown, Georgia. It ain't but 60 mile from Macon. We had two mules and a wagon, some plows, a grass mower, and a hayrake. One time we had use of a slave man and woman, Bub and Mamie. Wadn't our'n. They was *field hands* we borry from our neighbor. We put 'em up in a little shack next to our smokehouse.

How we git them slaves was, after Ma drop Lotta, Pa said hitch up the mules 'cause we goin' to see Mr. Morehouse. He live 'bout two mile east and had cows far as you could see. He didn't milk none of 'em. They was growed for eatin'. Every time a few git big 'nuff, they walk 'em to the stockyard and load 'em on a train headin' to Savannah. People say Mr. Morehouse was rich. He own six slaves, but I never seen all of 'em, least at one time. Fact is, he the only man I knowed even had no slaves a'tall.

Me and Pa talk to Mr. Morehouse 'bout how we in a peck o' trouble and could we please use one o' his field hands a modest bit since Ma sick in bed and she jus' dropped Lotta and we ain't got no way to git our work done. Well, Mr. Morehouse say 'cause we good folks, we kin use Bub till our crops is done. We was so happy we praise God all the way home.

The next day, me and Pa brung the wagon back to pick up Bub and his clothes and stuff. When we git there, Mr. Morehouse said he gonna do us a extry good turn and chuck in a Negro woman, Mamie, and it still won't cost us nuthin'. He said anyways, Bub and Mamie was kinda sweet on one 'nuther, and Mamie was soon to drop Bub's young'un. 'Nuther thing he said was Mamie kin pick a hamper o' beans faster'n nobody, and after she pick it, she quick to turn 'round and snap and cook 'em better'n any mama 'round here, and if our mama was to die from birthin', we gonna need a good kitchen hand. So, me and Pa figure that was good.

Strange thing was the Lustas ain't never had no slaves. We ain't even been aroun' no slaves 'fore and now we come up with two borried ones. Maybe we was headin' up in the world. I wadn't wrong, but it gonna take a spell.

It was closin' on down to almost fall and our crops was in so me and Pa put Bub and Mamie in the wagon and brung 'em back to Mr. Morehouse. Well, the man come right out and said would we like to rent 'em. Pa say he reckon, if it wudn't cost too much 'cause Ma still ain't well and how much is it? We talk some and Mr. Morehouse hem-haw and come up with twenty dollar a year for both of 'em, so we said OK real quick.

That year it come a bad winter and I was ten and the weather give us lot o' cold and rain and ice. Poor old Ma died 'cause she never git over birthin' Lotta and, beside, she git real sick on a bad case o' sposure. We didn't want two womenfolk dead 'cause o' one birthin', so we put in extry prayers for Mamie. Blest Pete, Mamie's little boy come out jus' fine and the Lord brung Mamie strong through it too. We kep' praisin' and thankin' the Lord for what He done for us. We knowed if we wudn't o' ask for special help for Mamie, she wudn't never o' made it.

So, me and Old Bob promise we gonna knuckle down and set our mind to workin'. I told him I be stickin' around to the end and he better watch close what he write down. I don't want nuthin' told that ain't come outta my mouth. Gotta keep my eye on that boy! He might be a hidin'-out Yankee spy. You know them Yankees. We shake hands and Old Bob laugh 'bout he ain't never shake hands with no ghost in his whole life.

Chapter 1

"The Young Volunteers"

©John Hill Hewitt

I never knowed much 'bout no war till I actual git in this'n. Bunch o' stuff sound downright crooked to me, but I ain't gonna talk 'bout it right now. I tell it as it come in the story.

Even after I quit bein' in the war, I still didn't know much 'bout it, 'cept it was terrible awful. 'Nuther thing is lotta Rebels, Yankees too, wadn't lucky. Word was, after the war git over with, countin' both sides, over 600,000 git theyselfs kilt. I usta be tolerable good at 'rithmetic, but I can't 'magine no number big as that. I always was sorry for them boys, all of 'em, and still am. God know this the truth.

I done some serious thinkin' 'bout war and figure out somethin'. Betcha it ain't never been no war had a full, honest, and sensible reason for bein' had. Only wars start is when two countries git a crow to pick with one 'nuther and they git to fumin' to meet up and settle it out. One I was in oughta had some people speakin' out. I reckon everythin' was gittin' too hot and steamied up.

Us boys in the army was jus' as bad. We git livened up and begin yellin' stuff like, "Yeh, man. I wanna go fight. I wanna die for Dixie. I wanna kill for Dixie. Send me in. I wanna fight them Yankees, even if some of 'em is my own kin."

Hold on. Less put them same shoes on 'nuther foot. If they was some folks from some other land cross the ocean wantin' to sneak over to our country and flat take us over and rule us, Blest Pete, you gimme a gun and I'll fight my britches off till I fall dead. All us would. Thass different. But I can't in no way figure out the whys 'bout the one I was in.

Some smart people 'round where we live talk 'bout how come this war happen. They say it was 'cause a big man from Illinois git 'lected to be president of us. He was Abraham Lincoln and folks say right outta the clear blue sky, he sidin' with them up North and puttin' the blame on us folks down South 'cause of everythin' goin' bad. He stir up a lotta stuff and wadn't long before, yep, you know it, a war done up and broke out.

All wars got a name. That'n did. Most people up North call it the *Civil War*. People down South call it the *War Between the States*. Reckon that what it was. But some folks 'round home call it best—*War of Northern Aggression*. Thass why in 1861, right when it start, I begin thinkin' I better go help out and run them worrisome creatures home. But one thing I wadn't gonna do. I wadn't gonna shoot none o' them Yankees in the back while they runnin'. Some o' them boys might be my own kinfolk. But if one o' them yellow belly sapsuckers turn 'round and point their gun at me, they deader'n a door nail.

Way Abe was talkin', we was sure he didn't like nothin' south o' the Mason-Dixon. That stripe my rear end without usin' no stick. Hey, we was born down South and we didn't cotton to gittin' our fine country in a mess. I love my land; my family's land. It was a little farm layin' southeast o' Macon, Georgia at a little place called Dodgetown. It was the best cotton-growin' land you ever saw. Thass where my pa and two o' his brothers join up in 1842 and plant cotton and grow 'nuff potatoes, corn, beans, turnips, and collards to feed three counties around us and maybe a whole Yankee state to boot.

When the Yankees shot them guns at Fort Sumter, ever'body 'round Dodgetown git swelterin' mad. That was our fort and ain't nobody, specially no Yankee, oughta be shootin' our fort. I kep' stirrin' my mind up tryin' to figure out 'bout it. It was the first o' June I told Pa I was ready to git up to Macon to see would they let me sign up. I git kinda sad when I seen tears in his eyes and he nod his head.

Wadn't hard to see how Pa feel. He never talk much 'bout it and begin stayin' to hisself a lot. Then one day, he up and said the newspapers was tellin' boys if they wanna be sure they gonna have a gun, they better bring one with 'em or they might be throwin' rocks. Pa reach up on the wall and hand me his best gun, the one us kids cudn't never hold. He give me a whole raft o' bullets, too. I git sad like he was.

I knowed I shoulda been leavin' out right then, but I 'cided to help Pa and Lack git in the crops first. I final start out on the middle day o' August, 1861. I won't never forgit the tears in his eyes when he said, "God bless you, son. Manage that gun like I would and like your grandpa would too. I know if Ma was livin', she be terrible proud o' you." Then he taken my hand and give it a good shake and said, "Boy, ever'thing now 'pend on you. Do what you oughta be doin'. But, don't do nothin' God wudn't like." My head drooped down more'n it ever done in my life.

So I left Pa and them and head up toward that big town. I ain't never seen no town big as that in all my time. Macon, Georgia. Some folks say 'Lanta was bigger but I'd soon not go nowhere gonna swallow me up worser.

I roam around that town and final git to the buildin' where folks say you sposed to go to join up. A man in a gray suit said to git in this line o' boys so they kin look at each one o' us, one at a time, but we gotta take off all our clothes first. Bless Pete, I ain't never raise up total nekkid in the middle of a big room where a whole raft of boys was nekkid too. Worse part, it wadn't no way I could turn 'way so they wudn't see me nekkid. Praise God they wadn't no nurses there.

'Fore long I git up to where the man in a gray suit was and he ask me what was my name. When I said, "Homer," he told me not to fool with him or I be in real trouble. There was this other nekkid boy standin' right side o' me. He was Billy Watkins and I figure he knowed more'n me. Billy whisper down low to me that them boys wearin' gray suits is Rebel soldiers and I sposed to say my real first name and last name and not jus' no nickname. And he said always say "Suh" so I change my mind quick-like and yelled out, "Homer Lusta, Suh." Land o' Goshen, I didn't wanna git in no trouble. Good old Billy. He straight me out real fast.

The next mornin' some more soldiers in gray suits taken us out to a field where they put us to doin' things like runnin' fast, climbin' over rocks, ridin' horses, climbin' up plow lines, wrestlin' one nuther, and liftin' big logs. They seen I was strong and could shoot a gun real good. I knowed how, 'cause I growed up on our place where it was my job to go out in the woods and shoot squirrels every day for breakfast.

The soldiers give us somethin' called a gun test. That was lotta fun. They said load your gun, jump up and twist around a whole turn, hit the ground standin' up, and shoot a rifle at a Yankee army hat settin' on a pole thirty yard away. I shot Pa's gun three straight times and hit that hat square on the hatband ever' time. They say my shootin' was just right and I was ready to go fight, so they put me in the CSA, the Confederate States Army, without no more trainin'.

They set me and Billy, who could shoot good too, and three other boys, James, Elliot, and Lawrence, to walkin' to a town called Milledgeville. They say that the State Capitol. I ain't never been there neither. We was gonna git more trainin' up there and then git ourselves joined in with a big bunch o' Confederate soldiers called a *company* and git after them Yankees.

They made Billy head o' us. I figure it was 'cause he was the smartest. They give him some papers to prove he was Billy and who we was. We sposed to foller him and mind what he say. They point over to the northeast and said if we go straight that way for sixty miles, we gonna run smack into Milledgeville. They give us a sack o' grits and some bullet packs and said shoot rabbits and squirrels if we git hungry 'long the way.

I was proud to be where I was. I was proud to be a Rebel soldier. I knowed 1861 was gonna be a good year for our side. I was double ready to fight for my land and my people. I was wishin' Pa, Lotta, and Lack could see me right now. Next time I see 'em, I gonna tell 'em how I feel today.

Chapter 2

"Bonnie Blue Flag"

©Harry Macarthy

It was gittin' cool weather when us boys was headin' up to Milledgeville. Us five new soldiers was gittin' more scared knowin' we was soon gonna leave and go fight real Yankees. I ain't never even seen no Yankee. None o' us ain't never went to war before. The graybacks give us some gray suits. They said it was Reb uniforms and we sposed to keep 'em, but don't wear 'em till we git up to the Reb base in Milledgeville. They said we liable to run slap in the middle o' some Yankees, and if we got them suits on, they might think we was Rebs and shoot us.

They give each one us a little bag look like a clothes bag. A soldier with three stripes on his arm call it a bindle. I ain't never hear o' no bindle before, but it look real nice. Kinda like a big handkerchief with the ends knot together to make a loop and you poke a stick through that loop. Then you sling it over your shoulder and walkin' is easy. Truth is, it look jus' like the little sack Ma usta give us when we walk over to spend the night at Grandma's.

The soldiers make us hide our gray suits in our bindle. They said we got to be real careful while we walkin' to Milledgeville, 'cause if we was to come up on some Yankees, we might be in a passle o' trouble. We ain't sposed to take them suits outta the bindle 'cause them Yankees might see 'em and think we doin' some kind o' Reb patrol and shoot us.

We git our stuff ready and left out 'bout noon. Most of us kep' talkin' 'bout how we was scared we gonna run smack in the middle o' some Yankees and git shot so we cudn't never go home no more. 'Bout that time I begin thinkin' I hadn't oughta joined up. Then I 'member how them Yankees was doin' us bad, so I figure I done right. I want Pa and Lotta and Lack to be proud o' me. And I knowed my ma is proud lookin' down from Heaven right now. I quit bein' scared; mostly.

We kep' walkin' toward Milledgeville, but we was slow goin'. The rain begin comin' down in sheets, like it wadn't never gonna rain no more. Gittin' toward dark, rain was still pourin' down hard. I was glad it was summer. Hadda been bad winter, rain like that wudda 'bout drown us and we wudn't never made it to Milledgeville.

We kep' walkin' cross this pasture, talkin' 'bout findin' someplace to git dry in and go to sleep, when we come to a fence and Blest Pete, a barn was nearby. It look like a cow barn with a fine roof and a bunch o' hay in it. It was dry inside it and we figure this where we kin rest and dry out. Maybe the next day, when we git up, the rain might be quit. Then we kin shoot us a squirrel or two, cook a pan o' grits, and git on up to Milledgeville and git after them Yankees.

We was lucky when, outta the blue, we hear a loud quacky noise. I set up and seen Billy Watkins, our leader, already standin' up, lookin' to see what was goin' on. Not more'n twenty yards 'way we seen a line of white ducks walkin' straight toward us. We figure they knowed where the barn was and was tryin' to git outta the rain too.

Billy told us to stay still and be quiet. He raise up his gun like he was aimin' to shoot. And thass 'xactly what he done. He must o' lined them sights up jus' right on that row o' ducks. Blest Pete, that bullet went through one of 'ems head and drop him dead. Then the dad blamed bullet kep' on goin' and drop the next one behind him too. Only thing I could think was, *Watch out, you dirty Yankee scum, wherever you be. Way Billy kin shoot, he gonna send all y'all headin' back north, squallin'.*

It was a hard time gittin' a fire goin'. Them little tin boxes the army give us to keep matches stay dry sposed to work good, but so much rain like we had, wadn't nothin' dry to light a match on. Hadn't been us findin' some dry rocks under the hay in the barn, we wudn't never lit no fire. 'Bout two hours later we had them two ducks clean and cooked, made us a pan o' grits, and our bellies was full. Wet as we was, we was ready to git some sleep. I kep' thinkin' 'bout how bad it wudda been if it wudn't been no barn.

Next mornin' we eat some left over grits and since it was near to daylight, we look 'round to see what was up 'head o' us. We didn't wanna bump into no mad farmer lookin' for two missin' ducks. We seen a little farm house out in the middle of a field, right the way we was goin'. Bes' we could tell, the yard fence was broke down. Most o' the windows was busted out and the yard look terrible growed up. We figure maybe nobody don't stay there no more. But the soldiers in Macon told us to be real careful and don't b'lieve nothin' nobody, special no Yankee, say. They said folks on the trail might think we was Yankees and shoot us 'fore we could prove who was right. When they said that, I started bein' scared this trip to Milledgeville was gonna be worse'n I thought.

Billy and us figure we better lay low and maybe jus' one or two of us oughta sneak up to the house and see if any folks in home. Billy pick me and Lawrence to be real secret, go up close, jus' look 'round, and come back and tell 'im what we seen.

The farm house wadn't really nearby so we walk up a fur piece more and sneak 'round bushes and trees so nobody wudn't see us. Pretty soon me and Lawrence was in the front yard. Both us look real hard and didn't see nothin' livin'. I told Lawrence since we ain't seen nothin' yet, lets go on up the front porch and knock on the door. He didn't wanna go, so I told him I would and when I walk up there, if he see somebody wanta shoot me, you shoot him first.

I raise my head up and look and wait. Then I walk to the porch. I still ain't seen nothin' movin' 'round yet so I walk closer. I git on the bottom step and watch the door. Pretty soon I git up on the porch and ain't nobody was pointin' nothin' at me. I knock on the door and listen. I knock again and put my ear up against the door and listen. *Ain't nobody here. I hope them Yankees ain't startin' to run our folks out from their houses.*

After all this lookin', I 'cided wadn't nobody in that house, or either they too scared to show up, so I wave my hand for Lawrence to come on up. Then I open the door so slow you couldn't hardly tell it was movin'. I couldn't see nobody in the first room, so I tiptoe in. I still ain't seen nobody, so me and Lawrence both look 'round some more. They was four rooms in the house and look like ain't nobody been there for a long spell. We didn't see no wood to burn or no food to cook or no clothes neither. There was some hickory nuts in a corner some squirrel musta haul in. We open the next door and a little mouse run to another room. Both o' them rooms had a bed without no mattress and look like ain't nobody been there for a long time. Me and Lawrence wonder did maybe the Yankees come in and take the folks away. Final, we figure we was safe and we got to go back and tell Billy.

Billy said we done a good job and we better be gittin' along 'cause we didn't have no idea if them soldiers in Milledgeville knowed we was comin' or not. If they knowed it and we was late we might git fussed at. Or they might think we Yankees and shoot us.

Billy told us one man need to go way up ahead and look out for Yankees. He said we gonna call him a *lookout*. That way all us wudn't run smack in to a whole raft o' trouble at one time. If somebody was to git kilt, might as well be jus' the lookout. Pretty soon we was movin' toward Milledgeville and follerin' Elliot, our lookout. Billy told Elliot if he see somethin' bad, hold a kerchief up and raise his arm up high.

I git to thinkin', *Was it gonna be this much trouble all the way to Milledgeville? Was it gonna be this kinda trouble to drive them Yankees all the way past Virginia? Was this war gonna be lot more'n we been countin' on?*

Things was goin' on pretty good for two hours. Elliot was still lookout, and we was follerin' Billy in a ten foot spacin'. I figure we oughta be in Milledgeville by tomorrow if nothin' bad don't come up. 'Bout time I thought things was goin' good, Billy said lay flat on the ground quick and look at Elliot. The boy was holdin' his handkerchief up in the air. Billy said he was goin' up to see if there was trouble and for us to aim our guns up that way and shoot if he said to.

Billy crawl and scamper past one bush after nuther, and then he set down side o' Elliot. They talk a minute and Billy git up and wave his hand for us to come up to where he was. We come up and seen we done run into a railroad track but wadn't no train comin' right then so we set down.

Elliot said while he was waitin', he hear some noise over to the right. It sound close to them tracks and might be some folks buildin' a barn or a house or somethin'. So Billy sent me walkin' 'longside the tracks over to the right and see what the noise is and don't git caught. Wadn't long till I spotted what the noise was. A sign next to the tracks, said, "GORDON." I seen some wooden buildings and one o' them was bein' built next to some tracks. It wadn't but a little ways to where them men was workin' so I went over and told 'em some o' my friends needed to git to Milledgeville and could we take a train up there.

"No, son," one o' the men said. "We tryin' to git them tracks fixed so trains kin run on 'em. If you was to try and drive a train now, the train could git real broke and you be in a double mite o' trouble. But you ask if you could take a train. Ain't nobody kin take no train. Them trains b'long to the railroad and can't nobody have 'em till they say." Them men start laughin'. I figure they was pullin' a joke on me.

I point back at my buddies. "Well, suh. Me and my friends is Reb soldiers and we headed north to fight Yankees. We got to meet up with our captain in Milledgeville."

Them men git to feelin' so down low, they start sayin' they sorry 'cause we got to go to fight and they didn't mean to be nasty or nothin'. They said to bring ever'body over to their buildin' and they gonna git us some food. Said they eat fried chicken and dumplin's a hour ago and they got a gracious plenty left over.

I come back and told Billy and them, and they start whoopin' and hollerin' and headin' down the tracks. We had a good time with them railroad men while we was eatin' all that good food and talkin'. We git to know 'em plenty good so I said to the leader man, "You mind if I write down a letter and you kin send it to my folks?"

"Yes you kin," he said. "Every night they come pick us up in a handcar and take us back to Gordon. You write down what you want on paper and I kin take it to old man Johnson at the train station and he kin send it on to your folks." So they give me a piece o' paper and a pencil and I write a message to Pa and told him we was goin' to Milledgeville to do trainin' and we was doin' fine and we ain't seen no Yankees yet and tell Lotta and Lack hey.

When that man said, *Gordon*, James jump up and told us his aunt live at Gordon and could all us write down a letter and could the railroad men take 'em to her so she mail it. "I know she a do it. She a nice lady," James said. "And tell her James say hey, too."

That head man told us the Yanks still runnin' the mail. We couldn't hardly believe it 'cause the Yanks and the Rebs ain't friends no more. He said we was right but they still haulin' mail right now, so we better send it now. We all sent a letter to all our folks. We taken up a collection and give it to the head man so he could give it to James' kin. James said his aunt would fill in more money if it wadn't enough. Then the head man said he was gonna make his men fill in some too. I git happy Pa and Lotta and Lack was gonna know I git in a good group and we OK. I knowed them other ones in our little group was happy too.

It was time to go and we said bye to them nice men. They point us the best way to go to Milledgeville fastest. After we left, I was sad 'cause they been so good to us. I thought 'bout how nice it be to work at a job like they was doin'. They got no Yankees worryin' after 'em. We all talk 'bout we was glad our folks was soon gonna know we fine.

Lotta stuff happen on this day, but we didn't git far. We come up on another little town and cudn't find no sign with a name on it. We figure we better keep up with where we was goin' and watch what out in front o' us 'fore we ram right in and git shot by Yankees. We move up to 'bout a hundred yards outside town. Billy set us up on a little dirt hill with our guns pointin' toward town and said to watch real close. He said if he run into trouble he gonna wave his arms and come runnin' toward us and for us to shoot who's chasin' him.

We watch Billy and talk 'bout the brave thing he doin'. The sun head to sunset when Billy go in a store. He stay a long time. We thought he shoulda done come out by now and we git worried. He never said how long to wait if he went in a store and didn't come out for a long time.

Then we seen him walkin' over toward us. He was wavin' his hand but wadn't runnin' fast. Wadn't nobody chasin' him so we didn't have nobody to shoot at. Then Billy begin wavin' his hand for us to come on up to him. We worry 'bout it might be a trick 'cause we hear all them stories 'bout how slick them Yankees is. I said I was gonna creep up to where Billy was and if I wave my hand friendly like, it was OK, so come on up.

I git up close to Billy and whisper, "You got trouble?"

"No, man. Git the boys up here."

I wave my hands kinda like I was paddlin' a boat upside down and them boys head our way. Billy told us he figure out we was in a little town name Coopers. All the folks 'round there said ain't been no Yankees here yet. The people in the store told us we was 'bout ten mile from Milledgeville and since it was gittin' real dark, we could go to a barn behind the store and we could sleep the whole night and not have no worry 'bout no Yankees. They said Old Maude, over next door, feed all strangers comin' through. They said since we goin' to fight Yankees, we don't have to worry 'bout scratchin' up no money.

Maude didn't have nothin' left but 'taters and some rabbit she cook this mornin'. That didn't matter 'cause it was a long time from when we was eatin' fried chicken and dumplins at Gordon and anyway this taste highly good.

We talk 'bout tomorrow when we sposed to meet them boys in Milledgeville. Maybe they tell us where we was goin' to fight Yankees. Everybody said we hope we all be in the same group. Things git real quiet and we was asleep in no time.

Dawn ain't hardly broke the next mornin' and most us was up and dressed and ready to leave. I git to thinkin' how nice these folks been to us. I hate leavin' here like I did at Gordon. Guess a heap o' good folks all over Georgia pullin' for us to run off them Yankees in a hurry. Then Maude pop up her head in the barn and said, "Who like grits?"

We started whoopin' and hollerin'. "Well, ya'll come on over." Grits wasn't all she cooked. She said one o' the men in town hear 'bout us gonna go fight the Yankees and he went out and shot two rabbits and she skin and cook 'em. Even got some coffee. That was some good eatin'.

On the way up to Milledgeville, all five us kep' talkin' more and more 'bout how many folks we run into is givin' us food and stuff and it's jus' cause we gonna fight the Yankees. We didn't have no doubts we was doin' the right thing. I git prouder every step I taken. I look at my buddies and seem like it was the same for them too.

The sun was straight up in the sky when we git to a town. We foller Billy on a street lookin' like it had must o' had lots o' people movin' 'round. I moved up long side o' Billy. "Watcha gonna look for, Billy?"

"Soldiers, if the Yankees ain't got 'em first."

We musta been in the middle of town now. So far, all the roads been goin' the same direction we was; north. Then I look up and seen some big streets start goin' east and west. "Billy, we got to be to the middle o' town now."

"Yeh, Homer. Let's see kin we find us a soldier and find out where we sposed to go. Y'all look 'round real good. I figure since this the capital o' Georgia, it woulda been heap bigger."

We move on through town. James said, "I don't know no difference in a Yankee soldier and one we gonna be, but look over there where them horses is tied up."

"I think them's Rebs. They got on gray suits," said Billy. "Let's go over and see."

All five us walked up to the soldiers. "Y'all Rebs?"

"Yeh. Who's askin'?"

"We new soldiers. Jus' signed up over at Macon last week and they sent us up to here to do trainin' and go kill Yankees."

"Ain't simple like that. But anyway go straight east and you come to a river, Oconee River. It's a big un. Then go two more miles and look over on the right. A big field with tents and wagons and horses and men. Can't miss it. Check in at the adjutant's tent. It got a red flag wavin' on top. Words on the flag say *adjutant*. I think he a major. Don't cut no shines with him. Say 'Suh,' 'Yes, suh,' 'No, suh,' and all that. Don't never set down when you nearbouts to where he is. Understand? 'Less he says to."

"Yes, suh."

"And don't say 'sir' to me, private. I ain't no officer. I got stripes on my arms. See? I'm a non-com. A non-commissioned officer. Now git goin'."

"Hey, boys," said James. "We got plenty to learn that ain't even 'bout shootin' nobody. If we gotta learn all this other stuff, how we gonna whip up on the Yanks?"

We walk east, 'cross the river, and the more we walk, the more soldiers we seen. They was on horses, wagons, and walkin'. The ones walkin' was stayin' close together, in little lines, with a non-com always yellin' at 'em. Then we seen the big field on the right, full o' tents, horses and wagons and men.

"There it is," said Billy. "Must be that tent. Got a red flag. Let's go find that major. Remember what we sposed not to do." They walked up to the tent. "Stop right here. I don't see nobody. Maybe I oughta walk in and tell him we here. Probably be real happy to see us."

Billy walk in the door to the tent. All of a sudden some yellin' and screamin' come outta the tent. Billy run out with a non-com chasin' him. "Boy, you stand here," the sergeant said to Billy. "You don't never jus' up and walk in a officer's tent. You wanna see the adjutant? You sposed come up to me and say, 'Sergeant, permission to see the adjutant, please.' Then you wait. Now try again and say it loud like I might be hard o' hearin'." The sergeant went back inside.

So Billy stand outside the tent door and said, "Sergeant, permission to see the adjutant, please." Boy was it loud. I bet it they hear it in Dodgetown.

A loud answer come back, "Git in here and stand front of this there door, soldier. Now." Billy went in. This time it musta work better. Nobody was yellin'. After a little while, the sergeant come out and line all us up and march us in. We give our papers to him and he taken all us out to the field and showed us how to pitch a tent and spread bedrolls. Then the sergeant told us since it's past sundown and we done walk all the way from Macon, for us to go to bed and listen for the bugle to git us up in the mornin'. He said first thing we gonna do when we wake up is how to put on our gray suits so everybody 'round here know we was soldiers and won't shoot us.

I git some good sleep. I thought 'bout Pa, and Lotta, and Lack and wish I could talk to 'em. If they could see me, I knowed they would be proud. I kep' hopin' they gonna git my letter soon so they know I was 'bout ready to fight them Yankees. I promise myself I was gonna work hard to be a good Reb.

Today is Ma's birthday. I remember it 'cause somewheres in my mind I remember she was born on September 10 and this is my mama's birthday. *Poor Ma.*

Chapter 3

"Cheer Boys Cheer"

©Anonymous

I git mad as a wet hen when that horn blowed. It wadn't even light o' day yet. Sound like it come from right outside the door. I jump up and there it actual was; right outside the door. Look like to me a little boy was blowin' it. He didn't look no bigger'n that baby boar hog we seen one time when we was pig-shootin' that cold night on the Altamaha River. Nope. Maybe he jus' out-stunted. They ought not 'llow no little kid like him marchin' 'longside us Rebs when we go git them Yankees. He might git kilt. I don't want no part in killin' a little kid.

We git up and put on them gray Reb suits. Mine didn't fit good and none of the rest of 'em didn't neither. We begin changin' and swappin' shirts and pants, tryin' to find out what fits. We was laughin' and makin' jokes 'bout which one of us looks worsest, when the sergeant come in our tent and started yellin' again 'bout how we sposed to already be outside with the rest o' our boys. He said when he yell, we got to *fall in* and do it fast. Yellin' must be his most favorite thing 'cause so far he done it a lot and he genuine know how. I 'cided I wadn't gonna yell none when they make me a sergeant.

Billy run out the tent first and I come behind. I seen a whole bunch o' soldiers walkin' 'round in little bunches. They was lined up pretty 'cause no matter what side you look at 'em from, they still in straight lines. The sergeant yell at us to git in somethin' called formation but I didn't know what it was and Billy and the others didn't neither. Lawrence told us he was so mad he was thinkin' 'bout up and quittin' and goin' back to Dodgetown. He said farmin' a lot more fun than fallin' in formation.

After he quit yellin', the sergeant seem to take pity on us. He calm down and git right kind hearted. He come over and taken hold of us, one at the time, and set each one 'mongst where them other boys was standin'. After he set us in a spot, he said where we was standin' was where we sposed to stand ever' time he say fall in. He told us to look up to the front of our group where a man was holdin' a flag up in the air and to 'member the stuff wrote on that flag. The big black number "9" mean we in the 9th Georgia Volunteer Infantry. The black letter "I" underneath the "9" means we in Company I. This mean Company I is part of the 9th Georgia Volunteer Infantry Regiment. That flag we lookin' at is a guidon.

"See that little yellow ribbon all by itself at the tip top o' the flag stick? If you look hard, you kin see a number, 151, wrote on the ribbon. That means 151 is your platoon number. So you boys in Platoon 151, Company I, 9th Georgia Infantry Regiment, so right now, start bein' proud of your platoon, and mostly, proud o' Dixie.

"We all in this here war as one, and one day any man standin' man here might save one of us, or he might git save by somebody. We ain't got no officers yet; no captain and neither no lieutenants. We sposed to git some soon, but right now I am the main leader."

By this time the sergeant was actual kind o' peaceful-like, and I was likin' him more and didn't matter how long it taken before no officers showed up. I think Billy and all them feel the same way. I was real glad he quit fussin' and begin showin' us how we sposed to act.

Final, the sergeant told us what his name was. I was glad 'cause I don't wanna be no friend with nobody I don't know. He said if we wanna talk to him, to stand up and raise our hand. Then when he answer, we call him either *Gunny* or *Sergeant Holmes*. he don't care which. It was right nice o' him to let us call him what we want. I figure I was 'bliged to do that since he done calm down. He said to look at all them men on that big field. We was jus' one company and the Regiment got three more out there. He said all them companies got their own guidon. We sposed to spot our guidon real quick so's if we start to fight Yankees and git lost, we kin git back quick.

Gunny set us runnin' 'round that big field two times so we git plenty exercise. He said we gonna do it ever' day so when we go fight the Yanks, we won't git too tired to keep fightin'. We taken a break and he begin tellin' us 'bout the army. He said it soon be chow time. I didn't know what chow was, so I git up and raise my hand and he said, "Speak, soldier?"

"Gunny, what is chow?"

Well, he said, "Ain't you never ate before?"

The whole platoon o' boys started laughin' at me again so I 'cided I wadn't never gonna ask no more questions. Next time I'm gonna wait and find out stuff I don't know by lettin' some other poor soul make a fool outta hisself. Anyways, Gunny final told us chow was food and we gonna git some soon.

Gunny put us runnin' again. I was 'bout to drop and Gunny said to stop runnin' and begin walkin'. He started sayin' things like "hut, two three, four" and then over again. All the men's feet was kind o' in a nice lookin' rhythm—all 'cept us five new boys. I figure we was gonna git fussed at again but we didn't. Gunny said, "Platoon! Halt!" I 'bout run over the man in front of me. Then Gunny yell out, "Column o' squads, first squad forward, route step to the chow line, march."

Funny thing happen. Them boys on the left side begin walkin' right behind one nuther. When they git to the end, the middle line started walkin' without not even bein' told. After them, the third line went by itself. Pretty soon it was jus' Billy and us new boys standin' there like a knot on a holler log. Gunny come over and said how come we didn't march too. He was kinda fussin', but pointed us to go on.

Well, I never seen nothin' like it. We end up 'long side some tables with a gracious lot o' food on it and all the boys was walkin' by it and puttin' food in little short buckets with handles. It was grits, ham, good old biscuits like I ain't never seen. I git me one o' them buckets and scoop some grits and ham. I laid down three biscuits in the food bucket and pour a healthy ration of cane syrup on two of 'em. Down at the end o' the table they was some little tin cups 'longside a big coffee pot. I begin thinkin' 'bout Pa and them and wishin' they was here.

Ain't nobody said no blessin' yet and Billy said it was kinda hard to say a blessin' when all these boys was tryin' to finish eatin'. He said everybody jus' say your own blessin' where nobody won't hear you. We walk over, set on the ground, and each one o' us said a blessin', and we cleaned ever' blessed bite off our food buckets. We seen some other boys who done finished eatin', bringin' their food buckets and tins over to a big water tub o' hot water and washin' 'em real good. So when we was finished, we done it too.

Gunny yell to fall in. After all that fussin' last time, we knowed jus' what to do. We seen our guidon and run over to our group. Gunny run up to us and said, "You learnin', boys. Forward march," and "Hut, two, three, four" over and over and Platoon 151 end up at a blank spot on the field.

Gunny told us 'cause they was some new boys here, we was gonna keep on workin' on how to march. Marchin' kinda turn to a fun thing for me. It was a good feelin' listenin' to ever'body on the whole field singin' songs like "Johnny Rebel" and "When Johnny Come Marchin' Home" and "Lorena" and specially when we started singin' "Dixie." All that made chills run 'round my spine and marchin' git a whole bunch easy.

Pretty soon Gunny guide us back to where we eat breakfast this mornin' and said, "Platoon! Halt!" We didn't have no doubt how to do it now. We been doin' it all mornin'. Before you knowed it, he said, "Column o' squads, third squad forward, route step to the chow line."

I look over at Billy and said. "Hey, Billy. Time to eat dinner again."

Billy, bein' funny like he always quick to do, said, "Nope. Time for chow again. You gotta say chow." I seen a bunch o' collards and some kind o' meat. We git closer and that meat turned out to be rabbits and squirrels all mixed together. There was sweet 'taters too, and some great big squares of the best lookin' cornbread you ever seen. I woulda thought my ma the one cook it, but wadn't her, 'cause she die three years ago. Even Lotta ain't no match for Ma yet, but she gittin' there.

They was more o' them little tins but this time they put some weak tea in 'em. But it had 'nuff sugar in it, so it taste good. Anyway, we been workin' hard and marchin' all mornin' and 'bout anythin' would taste good. All five of us git our stuff to eat and set down near a bush. It wadn't no time till our food buckets was empty and we was soppin' gravy with what cornbread was left.

Gunny yell for Platoon 151 to finish up eatin' and fall in. He said we gonna start practicin' how to scrap with Yankees and first we gonna learn to crawl 'round on the ground. We done it till it was makin' our gray suits terrible dirty. First we was crawlin' 'round on plain ground where there wadn't no bushes or trees.

Next thing, Gunny taken us over to where lots o' bushes and trees was. He split us in two groups. One group sposed to play Yanks and the other was Rebs. Gunny set it so the ones playin' Rebs would hide in the bushes and the Yanks try to find 'em. Next he made us swap places and do the same thing. We didn't have no real bullets so we jus' said "bang" when we seen a Yank. It got to be lotta good fun since we didn't have no real bullets but some of us started sayin' it be different when we usin' real bullets. It was kind o' scary to think 'bout stuff like that. He told us we was doin' tolerable good and we got to remember all the stuff we practicin'.

Outta nowhere come some loud music. We start talkin' 'bout it was a pretty song and we wondered was somebody gittin' ready to sing. Gunny told us the little bugler is the one playin' it. He said the song was "Call to Chow," meanin' when we hear it, chow is ready, but we don't jus' up and start runnin'. We sposed to wait for orders. We was glad that boy was playin' it 'cause we was hungry from a hard day.

Then Gunny said that bugleman got more pieces to play any time he want to. He said all of 'em got a diff'rent meanin'. He play somethin' for us to git up in the mornin' called "Reveille." One was "Taps", when we gotta go to bed. They was a few more, name of stuff like "Call to Arms," "Mail Call," and "Church Call."

Gunny say it was too many songs to 'member all of 'em, but the ones he jus' told us 'bout was the ones we gonna hear most. The bugler jus' played Chow Call, so we goin' to eat supper now, but we gotta listen up a little while after chow, 'cause he gonna play "Assembly." When we hear that, we sposed to fall in formation so we kin go do what we been doin' all day, but this time we was gonna do it in the dark. Billy said he guess the Yankees fight in the night too and not jus' in the light o' day, so we gotta practice that too.

It was good they give us chow 'fore we started doin' all that night trainin'. It was jus' like the dad blamed moon to be somewhere else in the sky 'cept over Milledgeville. I couldn't hardly see nothin', even after Gunny told us to look jus' where it was dark for over half a hour. He said it taken a long time for people's eyes to git used to the dark, but when it does, you kin see pretty good. I think he was right 'cause when we in the dark a long time, we kin see tolerable good.

We kep' makin' like we was in a real hard fight with the Yanks. I begin thinkin' how could I help my eyes see better. I didn't know nothin' that work right. Sometimes when I set back of one o' them bushes, and I knowed them boys playin' Yanks was comin' at me, I git scared 'cause I didn't see 'em. I git to thinkin' if I git scared when it wadn't no real Yanks, what was I gonna do when there was some real ones.

I begin thinkin' 'bout when Pa and Lack and me used to go huntin' for 'coons. We want a coon, we jus' turn loose Old Bean. That dog kin find a 'coon. And when he a long way off, you knowed jus' what he was sayin' with them different bark sounds. I git to wishin' I was huntin' with Old Bean right now 'stead of up here gittin' bit by ticks and redbugs and mosquitoes and no tellin' how many rattle snakes I done set down on and ain't seen 'em. Pa always said it don't matter 'bout a snake if you see him. Worse part 'bout snakes is when you don't see 'em.

I done all this thinkin' and clean forgit I was sposed to be lookin' for them boys sneakin' up. I guess I was kinda lucky 'cause I hear one of 'em crawlin' 'round on the other side of the bush I was settin' by. He was tryin' to sneak up on me so I jus' stuck my gun in his ribs and said **Bang** real loud.

Gunny raised hisself up and come runnin' over laughin' and hollerin' and said, "You doin' good, Lusta. Good job. That mighta gave you a medal if we wasta been fightin' the Yanks."

I feel good when that bugle man play a song tellin' us to march back to our tents. When Gunny turn us loose, I set outside our tent and look a long time at them bright stars. I said a prayer for my folks back home so they git 'nuff to eat, seed for plantin', and for no Yankees to come cross our yard. I prayed for me too.

Then I thoughta somethin' Ma usta tell us. She said 'cause we young uns, we still got a long life left we kin do lotsa good things in; things thatta raise up the Lusta name. "I can't no more," she said. "My young time done gone. But you chillun got time." Poor Ma. So I pray I kin be brave so I know jus' what to do when it come time to fight. I begin to tell God the same thing 'bout my buddies too, so I pray for all us at one time. I guess it don't matter none if I git two prayers and them jus' one. Best part of prayin' is I kin tell God what all us need. Ma always tell us God know anyways, but I jus' 'minding Him 'bout it. Poor lady. She was a good ma.

We was all learnin' a right smart 'bout soldierin' and fightin' and sneakin' up on somebody and, Blest Pete, we didn't have no idea we was learnin' that fast. Gunny said we was soon gonna start shootin' our guns and when we do, we gonna shoot at big targets made out o' paper with black spots on it. Then they gonna put up some big signs with a shape like Yankees and we gonna shoot them too. After we quit shootin', he gonna count up how good we hit them targets and each us gonna git a number he call a score, jus' like we usta git in school. I hope my shootin' score be bigger'n my schoolin' score.

Every now and then, a new man or two showed up and Gunny put 'em to work with our group. Sometimes a soldier with a stripe or two on his arm would come in. Gunny put one of 'em, Corporal Hinson, with our group and tell us he was squad leader. Sometimes he work us harder'n Gunny done and other times he set down and told us 'bout what gittin' shot at is like.

Knowin' how to do this stuff was creepin' on us, but kinda slow like. Maybe we kin teach them Yankees a lesson so they see we ain't no pushover. Best thing is maybe this war gonna be a tie and all us go on home in a day or two.

Gunny kep' all us runnin' out in the field. Sometime we work jus' in the day and lot o' times we run back out and run 'round at night too. Some days we work the whole day without not even stoppin' while we kep' on workin' the whole night. I git real sleepy them days.

One mornin' Gunny told us to bring our guns out to the field 'cause we gonna learn to shoot real bullets today. Thass what I been wantin' 'cause thass why I come here. Gunny git us in two little crowds. He taken one crowd and Corporal Hinson the next one. Gunny said our guns won't shoot nothin' till we put a minie ball and some powder in our gun and we laugh out real loud. Gunny git real mad at us. It musta seem we was makin' fun of 'im. He final settle down and told Hinson to go stick up them targets, ones with Yankee soldiers drawed on 'em, up on some pine trees.

We begin learnin' 'bout loadin' up them army guns. First thing Gunny showed us was put the back of the gun down on the ground and hold it on the top where the bullet come out. Then we pick up a paper bullet pack. Thass what holds the powder and the minie ball. Next we tear off the end of the bullet pack and pour the powder down in the muzzle and push the minie ball down in the barrel. Then we take the ramrod and jostle the minie ball down till it stop at the bottom. Last thing is pull back the hammer half-ways and put a firin' cap on this thing he call a nipple. Then when you full-cock the hammer, that gun ready to shoot. Gunny told us a practiced man kin load a minie ball in 'bout thirty seconds. I set out to learn it faster.

We shoot a whole lotta times that day. Corporal Hinson kep' takin' down targets already shot at and puttin' up new targets and marking down numbers. At the last of the day, the captain come out and look at all the numbers they been markin' down. Blest Pete, I come in best and Billy next. The captain shake my hand a whole heap and Billy too. I told the captain I been shootin' guns since I was a little boy, and I knowed I could shoot a heap good, but my little brother Lack, he kin shoot better'n me. Back home we git in our boats night and day and go roamin' up and down them rivers huntin' wild pigs and we always get a heap o' meat. Captain talk a heap 'bout what we done. I was proud.

The captain say all us boys done shot good grades and he was pleased a heap. I wudn't never believed I could shoot better'n nobody else. First chance I git, I gonna write Pa and them and tell 'em I ain't changed much and I kin still shoot a gun and I git to thinkin' I jus' might be the one gonna save the South, God willin'. But I don't know about Pa's gun. It ain't nowhere as good as them ones we got. I reckon I got to figure it out.

One day, Gunny told us 'cause we been workin' hard, we was gonna do some playin'. He help Hinson haul out some crocus sacks. I figure it was ear corn in them sacks when they dump 'em on the ground. It wadn't no corn. They was some little white balls and some curious lookin' wood sticks Gunny call bats. Them bats was 'bout three feet long and had a fat end and a skinny end. They was some great big leather things lookin' like big hands. Gunny said it actual was gloves and they was sposed to help us ketch balls. We kep' thinkin' why we wanna ketch no balls.

Gunny said we gonna play a game they call *baseball*. Him and Hinson begin markin' off little trails on the ground till it was a big square with four corners. They set a flat rock on one o' them corners.

Then they fill up three sacks half-full of sand and set one of them on each one of them three corners. They said them sacks was bases and the rock was home base. I ain't never hear of nothing called home base and cudn't figure why nobody in his right mind would never come up with somethin' like this.

They begin showin' us 'bout playin' baseball. They throwed a ball to us, one at a time, and we was sposed to hit it with a bat. If we hit it, we sposed to run 'round them trails, backwards by way the clock hands runs, far as we kin git without somebody pickin' up the ball and layin' it on us. If they lay it on us, they say they *put us out*. Best part is, if we go all the way 'round and step on that flat rock they call home base, and nobody lay the ball on us, we git somethin' they call a home run. Learnin' to play this game a lotta fun. I cudn't never 'cide how nobody ever come up with a game like this.

After while, it git to be the funnest game I ever played and I can't wait to git back home and show Lotta and Lack how to play it. After we make a baseball yard, Pa won't hardly git no work outta us.

So for a lot of days, first we go fight out in the woods, and do shootin', and then we come play baseball in our baseball field. It was better when we play baseball. Sometimes some o' them boys would git in a fight 'bout did somebody lay the ball on 'em or not. Gunny said save your fightin' for when we git up there and meet up with them Yankees.

The first day in October, Gunny git us boys together and say we done finish trainin' and we was goin' after Yankees real soon. He say we gotta be ready any day to move out. He didn't have no idea where we was goin' but we was gonna ketch a train. I was glad 'bout that. I ain't never rode no train. I ain't never seen but two, and one o' them was a 'long way off.

Gunny say nobody who ain't got a backpack yet to stand over to one side and git one from Corporal Hinson. It had belts and pockets and he show us how to fix it so we could cram it full o' stuff and walk a long ways and not git tired.

So every mornin' after we git up, I put my stuff in my backpack so I wouldn't be holdin' nobody back. We still done more trainin' and stuff and play baseball. At nighttime, we would send letters to our folks. I liked to set outside the tent and look at stars and wonder what Pa and Lotta and Lack was doin' right then. One thing I knowed was if they was lookin' at the moon right then, we was all lookin' at it at the same time. That make me git a sad feelin'.

I figure out one thing. Waitin' for somethin' we don't have no idea what it is or when it is, is hard to do. All the boys mostly said I was right. After a whole lotta days o' waitin', Gunny told us we was 'bout ready to go and fight, and we wudn't have to wait much more.

I git to thinkin' what Gunny said and that night I went out and set in the dark and begin thinkin' 'bout bein' back home, shootin' and cleanin' rabbits and givin' 'em to Lotta to cook for supper. I git this sad feelin' that stuff was 'bout to change. A real strong chill come over me and I wish I could see Pa and Lotta and Lack jus' one more time.

Chapter 4

"God, Save the South"

©Earnest Halpin & Charles Ellerbrock

.

Gunny hightail-it in our tent early one day sayin' how come we ain't up yet, and didn't we hear the bugle playin' "Assembly" and didn't we know that mean we better git up and out on the field right now 'cause we goin' to chow in a hurry and after that we gonna ketch a train. All us begin whoopin' and hollerin'. Like I said, I ain't never rode no train before. They ain't neither.

Gunny start to fuss 'cause we whoopin' and hollerin' when he was tryin' to talk to us. He said to git our gear in our backpacks and fall in formation with backpacks on and sling our guns 'round our shoulders and make sure they ain't loaded 'cause we don't want nobody shot that ain't no Yankee. So me and Billy and Lawrence and Elliot and James git in formation jus' barely time 'nuff to march to chow.

Somebody yell out, "Wherebouts we goin' on the train, Gunny?"

"I ain't got no idea, boys. 'Member what the captain said 'bout tellin' too much? The more people know a secret, the more chance the Federals gonna find out so they kin come and shoot us. So fall in formation. It's four in the mornin' and we gotta long day 'head o' us."

They made us a good breakfast. It was kinda like all the times before. They laid chow outside on the tables so we could jus' reach in and git what we want. Only this time it was so dark we had to git up real close to see what was fixed. It was the best eatin' I ever had—grits, big crispy biscuits like Ma used to make, and cane syrup. And Blest Pete, on top o' that, they give us big hunks o' fried ham. It looked like some we hack off a wild hog one time back home after Pa cook it on his roastin' rack the whole night.

I got no idea if the Army was gittin' better at cookin' since we git here, or maybe they jus' cookin' it better 'cause we gotta go fight the Yankees. But it was good vittles. Then we git to whoopin' 'bout we gonna whip them Yanks. After a little while, we begin talkin' in a low sad voice than the way we was used to. Some of us talk real low 'cause we knowed we all headin' somewhere, but some o' us not gonna come back. I got no doubt a whole lotsa prayin' was goin' on. Was with me.

Mornin' chow was soon over and that horn blowed again meanin' we sposed to git in formation. Gunny said the captain wanta talk to us. Most o' us only seen our captain maybe one time 'fore, so we was wantin' to see what he look like. Well, he come out to the front o' our company. Gunny saluted and said, "Company 'I'. 'Ten Hutt."

The captain git up. He stare us over real hard and start to talk. "Stand at ease, men. I want to talk just a few minutes about what we're going to do. Gunny said we are 102 strong, split into three platoons. Platoon 151 has 30 men. Platoon 152 has 31 men and so does Platoon 153. That means we have 102 tough and ready Southern boys who don't want their land messed with. We are the only company going from this base because we are the only company that has completed training. I watched you and believe you are ready. We will be leaving in the next half hour or so, so stay ready."

He talk real good. The captain hold up a little metal thing and said it was a whistle. He blowed it and it sound real loud. "This is a signal whistle," he said. "When you hear it, listen up, because something important is happening. Until we get to where the Yankees are, we'll use it to get your attention.

"We have a long march north to a place called Crawford Junction to catch our train. That's about a 45-mile trip. That's where our marching path will cross the train track. It'll be a tough march. We expect to get there about five 'o'clock tomorrow morning.

"But before we get there, we'll come to a little town called Sparta. We should be there about five o'clock tonight. The people who own Glen Mary Plantation are bringing us a big meal into town. They're probably cooking it right now. They're doing this because they appreciate what we're doing for them. It will be set up outside the Council House in the middle of town on some tables. Also a lot of local folks will be there to say hello and get us in the fighting spirit as we eat. And in case we might get hungry while we're marching on to Crawford Junction, they'll give each of us one of a paper bag so we can put some food in it to carry with us. But remember, we have to eat it all before we get on the train. We can't take any food on the train because they don't want rats climbing aboard with us. We will meet that train at five o'clock tomorrow morning.

"I don't know where the train is coming from, but it doesn't matter. We just hope the Yankees haven't gotten this far down yet. If they do and we are not ready, we could be in trouble. We must stay on our toes every minute, ready to shoot every blue coat we see.

"Men of 'I' Company, I am proud of you all. A few weeks ago most of you were out in the fields picking cotton or breaking corn. You have learned well. We're ready. I know we're ready. We will soon prove ourselves.

"We're supposed to have two lieutenants with us but they haven't been transferred yet from the battle at Fort Sumter. They're sposed to help Gunny and me give commands on the field, but we'll have to get along without them. So listen and do what we say as soon as we say it.

"Gunny, take command. And God bless you all, men."

Gunny blow his whistle and yell out, "Company, ten hutt." Then he salute the captain and call out "Company, route step, march." I was glad the gunny said *route step* 'cause we couldn't walk no 45 miles, stiff, like we was in a parade.

We was final movin' north. Me and Elliot thought them words the captain say was real pretty, even if we didn't know what some of 'em mean. Least we gittin' this war goin' and Blest Pete, we gonna run them Yankees back up North. It wudn't never be over if we didn't hop to it.

Walkin' up towards the north. I git to thinkin' ever' time my foot step on a new piece o' ground, it was one step I ain't done yet my whole life. Kinda sad to figure ever' step take me little bit more 'way from my home in Dodgetown.

I begin countin' up all the places I been to in my life. That didn't take long 'cause I ain't been to many. So I begin countin' all the places I ain't never been to 'fore. That was powerful hard 'cause I don't know all the places I ain't never been to 'fore. Then, I keep thinkin' 'bout some o' us boys right now in Platoon 151 wadn't gonna never git to go home again. Them other platoons the same. I don't know none 'o them, but they still Southern boys.

I begin prayin'. Prayin' is easy. My whole family done it all my life and most of 'em work 'cept the one we pray to keep Ma from dyin'. So I jus' pray kinda my own way and look up to Heaven and told God would He please be with us boys, 'cludin' me. I begin thinkin' again how it ain't no secret, specially from God, that some o' us boys is gonna git kilt. I ain't got no idea how God 'cides which boys kin come back and which ones gonna be scattered in bits and pieces 'round where we fightin'. I told Him I knowed it was a real big job He got to figure it out 'cause if I was one who was 'cidin', itta be too hard for my poor soul to bear.

After close to a hour, Gunny give us a command to halt. "Somethin' we got to do now," he said. "We gittin' closer to where Yankees might be so we gotta set out scouts. 'Member when we trained how to do this. Now we gonna do it for real. We got to git set so if the Yanks come close by, we gonna be safe case they attack."

Gunny git us in *scoutin' formation*. He put most of us in a great big group he call a main column. When we git back to marchin', the main column sposed to walk north in the middle o' the trail.

Then Gunny split the rest of us in four little groups of four boys each. He call 'em scout groups. One scout group sposed to walk out ahead 'bout fifty yards in front of the main column and the main column sposed to foller 'em. My friend Billy was in that group out front.

Scout group two 'sposed to walk 'bout thirty yards over on the left side o' the main column and scout group three 'bout thirty yards on the right o' the main column. The last scout group sposed to walk behind the main column 'bout thirty yards.

Gunny told all them scout groups to keep a check and see is any Yankees close around. If they was, the scouts sposed to whistle a signal and the scouts was to come runnin' back and join the main column and the whole company was to start shootin' at them Yankees. Gunny was extry smart to train us how to do that and Blest Pete, now we gonna need it.

Gunny blow on his whistle and yell out, "Company, forward march. Route step." After we git movin' the captain run up and start walkin' ahead o' the main column and Gunny went back behind the main column. I reckon Gunny was gonna git after any one o' us boys who don't keep up. By this time, them four scout groups hurry up and git in their rightful spots. It was full light outside now and we was natural lookin' like a bunch o' genuine soldiers.

After we been walkin' a while, we come to a big bunch of oak trees. Musta been a million acorns all over the ground. You couldn't put a foot down without steppin' on none. Elliot said look over to the right near them bushes. It was two deer and they was fatter'n a year-fed sow. Me and Elliot figure them acorns must be full of whatever makes a deer fat.

Elliot yell to Gunny could we shoot a deer and cook it when we git near the train. "No, we can't," said Gunny. "If we was to shoot a gun, the Yankees might hear it and come shoot us and we might not git to the train a'tall."

Me and Elliot keep talkin' 'bout how it was sad to leave all that deer meat. But we just keep marchin' and we plain forgot 'bout missin' out. It was soon the middle of the mornin' and we could see better. It wadn't no trouble seein' all our boys, front to back. Elliot was still walkin' near to me and he said wudn't no Yankee dare come up on us.

We kep' headin' the way the gunny said and pretty soon we run slam into a real wide creek. Ain't none of us could tell how deep it was, so Gunny git a boy to cut down a saplin' and stick it straight down and measure it. It come to over seven foot.

One of our boys in our main column said his uncle got a farm up near here and he went over to see him one time. His uncle tell 'em the name o' this little river was Oconee Offshoot and up here they got lotsa quarries and they full of deep caves and if you fall in one you might git sucked in it and you never git out. Ain't much need to try to measure it 'cause if we tried to, we might not never find no bottom.

So the gunny git two men to walkin' one way and two men goin' the other way to see if a bridge was close by. Wadn't no time they come back and said it was a nice bridge over to the right side, so the whole company march to where the bridge was and we all cross it. Some of them boys start throwin' rocks in it tryin' to make all us think it was fish jumpin'.

We cross lots more streams and a whopper of a big river. It was strange how big that river was, but it wadn't deep. Cold as it was, we cross it by jus' wadin' over. I didn't have no idea what was the name o' it since I ain't never been this far north before. Billy and most o' them other boys said they ain't been up here neither so I didn't feel too bad. In one o' them streams we seen some mighty pretty fish jumpin' ten a minute. It woulda been nice to stay here a hour or two, specially if I had a pole and some red wiggler worms.

If we wadn't headin' to war, it woulda been nice to jus' walk 'round and look at all that pretty land and them woods and watch them deer runnin' through the bushes and squirrels jumpin' 'round in the trees. Funny thing was, them squirrels was a whole lot more skinny than the ones at home. Guess maybe the Yankees been stealin' their nuts and stuff.

Gunny blowed his whistle said it was time to stop and take a rest. I was tired so I jus' laid right down on the ground and it wadn't a whole minute till I was close to sleep. I begin thinkin' 'bout goings on at home. Good thing the crops is in 'cause it take strong help to bring 'em in. My mind conk right out so I guess sleep take hold o' me.

It didn't seem like no time a'tall when Gunny yell again and say we gotta git on the way or we might not ketch the train. Only reason I was on his side was I want to see what ridin' a train is like, 'cause I ain't never rode none.

Then we was back on the road and the main body was headin' north. Gunny put me in the front scout group and I was glad. My eyes is good and if a Yankee is out there, he gonna ketch one o' my bullets right in the head. Goin' was pretty good. Ever' now and then we come to a deep ravine or a river we can't cross, so Gunny had to figure out the best way to go. It come to my mind I might git to be a gunny someday so I set out to learn all I kin from the gunny we got.

Some of us up front talk 'bout we was tired and we need a rest. Well, Gunny must not been thinkin' that way so we kep' on goin'. We git to passin' through some real thick woods. Some of 'em got big quarries and we had to figure out how to go 'cross. Mostly, it was Gunny who figure it out so we was glad he was leadin' us.

Gunny yell we gonna take a break, but first all us come over and sit in front o' him and listen. "Sit down, soldiers," he said. "You doin' real good. Right now it a little past ten o'clock and we makin' good time. We gonna take a 15-minute break right now and you kin roam around a little bit and shake it off. But don't git away too far. Watch out for Yankees. We still got a long way to go 'fore we git to Sparta where we gonna git some good food."

Billy and me walk around some and Blest Pete, we found somethin' good. It was a pine tree weighed down with bullis vines and a few maypop vines growin' on 'em. I ain't seen that many ripe bullis grapes and nice yellow, ripe maypops my whole life. Billy said run tell Gunny what we found and wadn't long everybody was crunchin' down on sweet muscadines and suckin' out maypop juice.

The captain come over and said what was we doin' and we showed him. He ask would it make us sick and I said, "No, suh. Hadn't never yet in my whole life."

It was somethin' real funny 'bout that captain. When we told him we don't git sick, he pick off a handful of them bullisses and bite in 'em. They musta taste good 'cause a smile break out on his face so he crammed some more in. Then Billy give him a maypop. He tried eatin' it but it wadn't easy. He tried anyway. Most us talk about this was the first time we ever saw a captain laugh. Right then, me and Billy figure we was gonna fight hard and do whatever our captain say. Guess he jus' like us, 'cept he got three bars on his shoulder.

Most the boys was sayin' they was sorry to hear Gunny blow that whistle, but I was ready to git on up to where that train is 'cause I ain't never rode none 'fore. We been goin' a long time and most of us was real hungry 'cause it been a long time ago since we eat. Gunny said we 'bout six hours from Sparta, and that mean we got 'bout 15 miles to go. I git to hopin' them plantation people was done cookin' all that food just like we like it.

We kep' askin' could anybody smell food yet. Elliot say he did and it smell somethin' jus' like hog ribs, but nobody paid him no mind. Blest Pete, that boy ain't got much of a mind no way. Most of us hope the captain and the gunny ain't gonna give him no real job in the war. Do and we bound to lose.

Gunny kep' on blowin' his whistle 'bout every hour or so and sittin' us down to rest. He said we gotta learn to git up energy. Up to me, I'd soon keep right on walkin' till we see them food tables. Closer we git up to where we was goin', the walkin' git harder. Some of the boys say it was 'cause we goin' uphill. All of us was lookin' to the day when the war quits and we come back this way. We begin cuttin' little slices in tree bark so when we on the way home we kin say *we come this way*. Then Gunny make us stop cuttin' tree-marks 'cause Yankees might foller us to Sparta.

We kep' sayin' ever' step we taken git us closer to us eatin'. One o' them smart boys name Hal marchin' with us say we was crazy. He told us everybody know if you keep marchin', you git closer. And stuff like how come we tryin' to teach everybody somethin' they already knowed?

We said we know all that, but it jus' somethin' we was sayin'. All us boys knowed Hal was jus' lookin' for some kinda way to put us down with. Reckon he think he better'n us. Maybe he jus' hopin' Gunny gonna hear him and think he extry smart and give him one o' them stripes to go on his arm. I prayed a bunch and told God don't let Hal be no boss o' us.

Chapter 5

"Good Ol' Rebel Soldier"

©Major Innes Randolph, CSA

After all that fast marchin' and restin', Elliot say he seen a big tall buildin'. I look real hard and seen it too. Best I could tell this far 'way, musta had three floors in it. Gunny blowed his whistle and told the scouts to stay right where they was and don't move.

Gunny come up and look 'round at us boys in the main column. He point at four of us. One of 'em was me. I ain't had no idea how come he point at me and I figure it wadn't gonna be nothin' good. Didn't take long to find out. He said them he point at was gonna be a patrol and we gonna sneak up on that town. I was final happy 'bout somethin'. I was a patrol. Since I ain't never been no patrol 'fore, I gonna write a letter to Pa and tell 'im I been a patrol. But I ain't gonna write no letter till I find out what a patrol do.

Gunny told us to go up close to that town and see have we come to the right place or not. "If it ain't Sparta," said Gunny, "then find out what and high tail it back. And don't shoot at nobody 'less they shoot you first. If it is Sparta, it mean we git the right town, so sneak up closer and see if any Yankees is pokin' 'round. When you find out all that stuff, make like a rabbit and git back here fast."

I ask Gunny how we gonna know if we see a Yankee? I never seen one my whole life. Well, Gunny throwed his hands up in the air. He musta git upset, but I didn't see no reason why jus' 'cause I ain't never seen no Yankee.

"Lusta," he said with his eyes starin' at me real hard. "You know you ain't gonna plain walk up to a Yankee and ask him is he a Yankee. You hafta sneak up so he don't see you and see is he a Yankee. Now I'm gonna teach you right now how you know a Yankee. Ready?"

"If we gonna be a patrol, we gotta know, Gunny."

"Look at your uniform, Lusta. What color is it?"

"Look like kinda gray."

"OK. You done hear me and the captain talk 'bout grey coats and blue coats. Right?"

"Yeah, Gunny. I ain't figure that'n out neither."

"Well, if you look up and see somebody wearin' a blue uniform and you got on a gray one, and if we call the Yankees blue coats, which one you think is Yankees?"

"I reckon the blue suits is Yankees."

"Right. Now, somethin' else. If the man in the blue suit a Yankee, and you got a gray suit on, what kinda soldier that make you?"

"A Reb, Gunny?"

"OK, ever'body clap hands for Homer."

I git happy 'cause I was doin' good. I 'bout cried right where I was standin' when I hear them boys clappin' for me. Then I wish I could find some paper and write Pa and them a letter and tell 'em I was gittin' to be a good soldier 'cause them boys clap for me and I was gonna be a patrol and maybe our captain might soon gimme a stripe on my arm, even 'fore Hal git one.

Gunny set Gerald head of our patrol when we git ready to move out. "Whatever Gerald say, you do, without no fussin'. And don't stay long. First thing, figure out if that town is Sparta. If it is, see if some Yankees roamin' 'round. If it ain't Sparta, find out what and run back quick. Go."

We walk toward that big tall buildin' 'cause it probly was in the middle of the town. Gerald put me up front to stay 'head of the rest of us 'bout the distance a good dog kin run in ten second. He say jus' one boy harder to see than a whole raft of people. We got to find out where we was. If it ain't Sparta we got to find out what is it and run back 'fore we git shot.

I set on a straight line for that tall buildin' and pretty soon I seen a white tower not high as the tall buildin', but nearbout. I stare real hard and seen somethin' wrote on the tower but I wadn't close 'nuff to make it out 'cause them letters was faded out bad. When I git near to it, the stuff wrote on the tower was jus' right: S-P-A-R-T-A.

Then I run back real fast and told Gerald and he said I done a good job, 'cept did I see some Yankees in town? Well, I told him I was so glad to see we was at Sparta, I forgit. So he sent me runnin' back to see could I spot some Yankees.

I git back up to where I was and look 'round for somewhere to spot blue coats from. I walk aroun' in the back of a bunch of stores and come up on one with a ladder goin' to the roof. I climb up that ladder real quiet-like and look down at the street. There was people goin' every which way and so far, ain't nobody seen me, so set I set down on some bricks so I could look over the edge and git some rest too.

It was a real long time and I ain't seen nobody wearin' no blue coat 'cept in a little while this kind o' pretty lady come out of a store wearin' a coat. First I thought it was a blue coat, but I look harder and seen it was a black coat. That black coat kinda look like a blue coat so I figure I better keep lookin'. She was real pretty and that black coat was black like the sky at midnight. She had on a white shirt under it and them two colors set that lady off somethin' pretty. I kep' on starin' at her. She was talkin' to all them people, 'special the men, and they was payin' her lots of 'ttention. I wish I could talk to her, but I reckon I can't, 'cause I'm a patrol. So I set back down on them bricks, but I kep' my eyes on her mostly.

Wadn't long 'fore I git to wanderin' how long I gotta stay up on this roof and look for Yankees. I musta been here a whole hour and figure I better git back and tell Gerald. I git on the ladder to come down, but I was so tired and ain't had nothin' to eat, I plain give out and fell down to the ground. A fat lady was comin' 'round the side of the buildin' and she scream, "Yankees are comin'." It was so loud Pa coulda hear it all the way to Dodgetown. A man come runnin' up, holdin' a gun in his hand. He point at me and said, "Hands up." I put my hands up. I ain't never had to put my hands up 'fore. I musta done it right 'cause he didn't shoot me.

I seen the man with the gun was wearin' a shiny star on his shirt. He say he was a constable. I didn't know what that was so he told me he the law. I knowed what that was. He put me in jail and begin askin' stuff 'bout was I a Yankee spy and was this town 'bout to be in menace. I kep' tellin' him I was with the Rebs and we was jus' outside of town and sposed to come eat supper tonight. The constable said he was gonna find out about this and I better be tellin' the truth or I might not never see the light o' day no more.

In no more time than it take a quail to git from full stop to full flyin', that constable come runnin' back in and said his name was Harold, and I could call him Harold. He said I was tellin' the truth and me and him was goin' to where my Rebs was and tell 'em we wadn't in no trouble.

When me and Harold come back to where Gerald was, them boys kep' sayin' "Halt" and sayin' why was two people comin' from that way when it sposed to be one. I kep' yellin' to Gerald that Harold was our friend and quit makin' noise. Gerald final figure out we was the ones who been hollerin', so everybody git to bein' such good friends with Harold, and we all begin shakin' hands and havin' kindness to one another.

Gerald said since we done found out everythin' was fine, and we was endin' up real good friends too, he was gonna send a man back to tell Gunny. Me and the rest of our patrol set down on the ground and Harold did too and we begin to talk about things we was hopin' they was gonna give us to eat tonight.

Little bit later here come the gunny and the captain and they say we done a good job. I was plenty proud now and I wish I could find some paper and write a letter to Pa and them. I didn't have no paper so I jus' figure I got to 'member all the stuff so I kin tell 'em.

Gunny got us boys in a good formation and yell, "Company, attention, forward march, route step." He kep' yellin' while we was route-steppin' and said he knowed we was tired and hungry but we was gonna git in a good-marchin' mood for comin' in town. When we git closer we gonna put Harold up to the front o' all us boys and we gonna change from route step to real marchin' step. He say we need to look like we come from one o' them army schools. He give us what he call fair warnin' 'bout any boy messin' up our marchin'. Truth be, that boy ain't gonna have a blessed bite to eat. I 'cide I better march real good 'cause I ain't had nothin' to eat for a passle o' time.

Little while later, Gunny call Harold up to the front. They begin talkin' and Harold was pointin' this way and that way. We git to marchin' in the middle of the road and Gunny yell out, "Company halt." Well, we come to a halt and then Gunny yell, "Y'all march bes' you ever done. Company. 'Ten Hutt." Well, we come to attention and then Gunny said, "Forward March" and begin to count, "hup two three four," just like when we was marchin' in Milledgeville. Gunny said he thought it was somewheres close to five o'clock and Harold was gonna lead us to the Council House.

We kep' marchin' and the road we was walkin' on turn to a real smooth street. It was easy to march on, so we begin to look a smidgen better now. People show up all 'long the side of the street and start wavin' Reb flags at us and whistlin' and yellin' good things at us. Little boys was marchin' 'side of us holdin' sticks like they was real guns. Chills come over my back.

We come to what musta been the middle of town and seen this brick buildin'. Gunny yell we was almost to the Council House and look real sharp. Wadn't no trouble. We was already straight as a arrow. By now, Harold was up front of us marchin' right beside the captain. Harold point over to the right and Gunny yell, "Column right, march."

There it set. Jus' what we been waitin' on since we eat this mornin'. A real good smell come from all them tables with food on 'em. Ladies was wearin' long dresses with aprons and hats. All us boys was oohin' and aahin' at the glory sight we was beholdin'. I even seen that pretty lady in the black coat and white shirt and I made my mind up when I git to eatin', I was gonna tell her how pretty she look.

Gunny said, "Company halt. Stand at ease." We all halted and Gunny begin to tell us all 'bout bein' mighty polite and sayin' thank you and ma'am and suh and please. We was not sposed to slurp tea and drop no food on the ground and don't chew with our mouth wide open. We was not sposed to fill up our plates too full. He said git one o' them cloth napkins and hold it in our hand and wipe our mouth all the time 'cause if you eatin' food and it smudges on your chin or sticks 'round your lips, it makes people wanta go throw up.

I knowed all that 'cause Ma and Pa always told us. I git plenty of licks 'cross the backside when I forgit. I kep' hopin' I could 'member what Gunny was sayin' 'cause I might see that lady in the black coat. I hope I kin think up some good things to say. I hope she don't run away when I say somethin' to her and make all them boys laugh at me.

The captain told us don't say one dad blasted thing 'bout where we goin' and where we come from. He said if we was to start tellin' all 'bout us, the Yankees might figure wherebout we goin'. We told the captain ain't none o' us know where'bouts we goin' anyways, so we can't tell nobody nothin'.

Gunny final git up to the front and said it was time to git in line and don't push and be extry nice while we eatin'. "And when we all done eatin'," he said, "ain't one single boy better not forgit to say thank you to everybody you see. And say it in a kindly way. These nice folks done work a whole heap fixin' all this stuff. We want 'em to know we thankful what they done and we aim to fight off them Yankees all we worth."

If I don't never 'member nuthin', I gonna 'member this gatherin' for a lotta years and probly my whole life. I ain't never eat no food taste so good like that. Whoever fix it was the best cook ever was. Gunny musta thought the same 'cause he fill up his plate with fried chicken and rice and gravy and snap beans, and top it off with corn bread and ice tea. He was doin' jus' like he told us. He didn't drop no food. Wadn't no food hangin' on his beard and he ain't slurped a sip o' tea.

The captain was havin' a good time too. He was mostly talkin' to some men who was walkin' 'round wearin' suits and white shirts and ties. One of the boys in our company say he seen the captain when this lady come up to him and taken his empty plate and give him another one full o' banana puddin'. Some us boys said it must be good to be a captain and git brought food. Gunny said that lady was Mrs. Beckum and her husband was mayor of Sparta. I can't wait to tell Pa and them I seen a mayor and I ain't never seen one 'fore in my life.

We kep' watchin' all this goin' on and 'fore you knowed it, that same lady in the black coat and white shirt come up and stand right side o' the captain. Me and Billy sneak over nearby to where we could listen at what they was talkin' 'bout. She was askin' a lotta questions like where we was goin' and was we gonna ketch a train and how long we gonna stay. I kinda git worried over what he was tellin' her. He was sayin' all kind o' stuff. I ain't hear a lot of what he was sayin', so I whisper to Billy what I was thinkin' and Billy listen a minute and said he was scared too. Me and Billy said why don't we just watch a while and make sure ain't the captain sayin' too much.

The lady and the captain kep' talkin' some more and he went one way and she come traipsin' over nearbouts to where me and Billy was. I was right. She was plenty pretty and I git scared she was gonna stop and talk to us. I ain't never talked to no lady pretty like she is. I kinda turn my back to the way she was walkin' and then she come right up to us.

"Hello, boys. Are you havin' a good time?"

"Yes, ma'am," Billy said. "Y'all really got some good food."

"What's your name?"

"Billy, ma'am."

And just where is such a good looking young man such as you from?"

"Way down south o' here, ma'am."

I was proud of Billy not sayin' nothin' she could figure out.

Then she looked at me. "And what's your name, soldier?"

"Homer, ma'am."

"Are you boys going to catch a train?"

Billy was over to the side shakin' his head no, so I said, "Nobody ain't told me nothin', ma'am." I said that 'cause my ma usta say I can't tell no lies, special to a lady, so I couldn't say 'no'. I figure what I said was best.

"You don't know? When I looked at you, I liked you very much. I saw those good looking eyes and I thought you must be a lieutenant or maybe even a major."

"No ma'am. I ain't nothin' but a private."

"Shawsh. You're just being modest."

"I reckon, ma'am."

"Well, boys, I know what brave soldiers like. I know you haven't been around very many nice young ladies recently because of this war."

I 'cided I needed to say somethin' fast. "No ma'am, we ain't. Fact is, ma'am, I ain't never been 'round no nice young ladies."

"Billy and Homer, you are my my friends. I know some young ladies in town who would like to meet a couple of handsome warriors. Would you like me to introduce you to some who are very, very lonesome? Would you like that? Your captain doesn't have to know."

Right quick I said, "Yes'm I would."

"Then be real quiet and follow me through that peach orchard and when we're out of sight, we'll go down to a house on Boland Street and meet some special friends. You'll like them a whole lot. You are men. They are women. Just wait and see what they can do for our Rebel fighters. They like to be close, if you understand what I mean."

I told Billy to come on and let's foller that lady. "I gotta see what she talkin' 'bout."

"Homer, you crazy. She ain't tellin' no truth."

"She ain't lyin', Billy. She wudn't say nothin' like that 'less it true. She too pretty."

"Homer, you're crazy. She can't be tellin' the truth. If the army was to ketch us, they have a rope 'round our neck in no more'n a minute."

"Nobody ain't gonna know. I ain't never been close to no girl. You hear what she say. They jus' waitin' for us."

"Homer, you know that lady ain't tellin' the truth."

"How come she would say a lie? Ain't no way that pretty lady gonna tell no lies to us Reb soldiers. We on her side."

"We better tell Gunny."

"You gonna mess it all up, Billy. I ain't never had no chance like this and you gonna mess it up. If you ain't goin', then I do it all by myself and when I come back I tell you all the fun I had."

I run up and told that lady I was goin' with her and she told me to hurry right now 'cause the ladies are lonely. Billy yell loud at me to come back. The lady say don't pay no 'tention to Billy 'cause he's jus' shy and wudn't have no good time anyway. We git down to the street she said was Boland Street and she point at a house with a big rock in the yard and we run up on the porch.

"Open the door for me, Homer. I can tell you're a gentlemen who always open a door for a lady." I open the door real wide and let her go in first. Then I come in and shut the door. 'Bout that time some big men grab me and drag me in this room near the back o' the house. They tie my hands and set me down in a chair. A man in a green coat pull another chair right in front of me and begin askin' things.

"Are you a Reb soldier?"

"Yes, suh." The way that man talk was plenty strange. I couldn't hardly understand his words. I figure he musta been from China or New York or Hawaii.

"Where were you before you came here, Homer?"

"Didn't have no name. Where I lived was way out in the country till I went to the army."

"Where did you go to join the army?"

"I don't 'member what was the the name of it."

"I don't believe that. Where did you do your training?"

"You ain't bein' fair. That lady in the black coat told me I sposed to git to know a lonely lady."

"That comes later."

"Then I ain't sayin' nothin' till I see them ladies."

"I'm giving you thirty seconds to answer my question. Where did you do your training."

"I ain't sayin'. That lady didn't say I have to answer no questions first. I wanna see that lady."

'Bout that time the man in the green coat slung somethin' and hit me in my face and I didn't hardly know nothin'. I reckon I was sleep 'cause when I come to, he was pourin' water on my face. I couldn't see straight. I ain't never git whack like that.

"OK, boy. I'm asking you once more. Where did you do your training?"

"I told you I come here to see some ladies and I wanna see them ladies."

Whatever it was that man hit me with first, he hit me again with it or somethin' else jus' as bad. I don't 'member nothin' 'cept when I come to, Gunny and ever' one of Platoon 151 was half-killin' them strangers. They was shacklin' their arms and legs and chainin' 'em to a tree out in the yard. I wadn't very steady but Billy help me walk behind the rest.

"Homer, them's Yankees. I git hold o' one o' them men and told 'im he was gonna talk or I was gonna twist his neck off his body. I 'bout done it too, till he begin to spill his guts.

"He said them six men is real Yankee spies and the lady in the black coat usta be a Reb lady spy. She live in New Orleans now. Her name is Pauline and she switch sides and start workin' for the Yankees. She tryin' to git some Reb ladies 'round here to be spies too. We was messin' around and makin' one o' men talk, and she jus' up and git away and we can't find her, but them six men is in trouble. The one talk is goin' to jail and the others gonna be shot."

Gunny come back to where I was and he say he oughta do what the man in the green jacket done to me ten times over. He said he talk to the captain but he ain't gonna kick me out or give me no court-martial. "But next time you do somethin' like this, you gonna wish you'da been born a lady. Understand?"

I told the gunny don't worry 'bout that and I done been taught a big lesson.

"I hope so," Gunny said. "Right now we gotta git movin' and ketch up to the company 'cause we gotta ketch a train."

"Gunny, I lost my gun."

"I know you lost your gun. And guess who got it. The captain. And he say if you want a gun when we git up there to meet them Yankees, you gotta see him. You gonna have to say how come you lost it and how you gonna make 'surances you ain't never gonna let no gun git away from you."

"Kin you jus' tell 'em for me, Gunny?"

"No. The captain want to look you straight in your eye."

"When I gotta go talk to him, Gunny?"

"Captain say you pick the time."

Chapter 6

"Goober Peas"

©A. Pindar

I high-tail it back to the Council House with Gunny a inch 'way off my tail. The food still on the table. Billy and Elliot come over say the rest of our company was gone. They head northeast toward a little town called Powelton 'bout 15 miles away. We sposed to ketch up with 'em by the time they get to there.

"Hurry. Fill up a food bag," said Billy, "We gotta go."

"I hate to ketch up 'cause I gotta see the captain and get my gun back and I'm know he gonna chew me out down to a hub."

"Better do that than run," said Billy.

"What happen to them spies on Boland Street?"

"Gunny told me they put one o' them monkeys in jail and the firin' squad taken care o' the rest. They soon be turnin' up daisies."

"I wish I coulda seen that. How 'bout that pretty lady?"

"They still lookin' for her. That constable in Sparta gonna send a telegraph back to Milledgeville so they kin tell somebody big what she done."

Gunny and me fill up two paper bags apiece with some food. Mostly it was fried chicken 'cause I kin carry it better and 'cause fried chicken taste better'n greens. I sneak and eat some right off the table while I fill my bag up. I kep' wishin' I could get Pa and Lotta and Lack up here right now. They wudn't never believe all this I been eatin'. And poor old Ma. She in her grave now and ain't never had no chance to eat no food like we eat. 'Cept all that good stuff God got in Heaven.

Me and the gunny and Billy and Elliot final head out for that little town to the northeast call Powelton. The rest of the boys git a big head start. We knowed when we git to Powelton, we gonna rush on to Crawford Junction to ketch a train at five o'clock in the mornin'. I don't wanna miss it 'cause I ain't never rode no train. We begin walkin' faster to ketch up. Gunny say if we keep up with him, we kin make it.

The moon up in the sky was full blowed size. I always like walkin' in the dark with that kinda moon. I ain't never figure why sometime the moon is a slim moon and then a few days later it turns fat and moves 'round and 'round the sky. The sun don't do that. Always been peculiar to me how come them two ain't already bump in to one 'nother. I ain't never been able to figure out stuff like that, but I reckon it's true 'cause I know God know why and He ain't the kind o' man to play no foolish tricks on us folks down here. I hope He don't. I been believin' in Him all my life and I don't think nobody I believe in gonna double-cross me.

We been fast marchin' for a long time now and kep' lookin' up ahead. Elliot let out a yell, "Look yonder. There's some people. I see 'em in the fog."

"Yeh, I see 'em," Gunny said. "Billy, you and Homer sneak up close and see who it is. Don't let 'em see you till you know who they is."

We walk up close and soon git 'bout on top of 'em. I told Billy it looked like that one over on the left was Lawrence. Billy said to sneak close and raise my hand if they was them. I git so deep down in that grass I knowed how a worm feel and, Blest Pete, I hear the captain talkin' so I told 'em I was Homer and I wadn't no Yankee. They pat me on the back and I run back to tell Gunny.

In a few minutes, we all git back together 'fore we git to Powelton. The captain told us all to sit down a minute. He said it was nearbout four o'clock now and we gonna walk right on to Crawford Junction and ketch the train 'bout a half an hour later.

I run over where the captain was and I ask him could I have my gun meetin'. He said OK and start fussin' at me and said I oughta be gittin' a court-martial, but he wadn't 'cause I didn't answer none of them questions that Pauline lady was askin'. The captain git kinda nice. He gimme my gun and begin braggin' on me 'cause I didn't tell no secrets. He say anyway, he gonna need me when we fight the Yanks 'cause I kin shoot good. I wish Pa and Lotta and Lack coulda hear him say that, and Ma too, but I guess since she done gone to Heaven, she saw me do it.

I kep' on lookin' up at the moon movin' over to the west and it was gettin' pretty far down in the sky. I figure it was gonna be sunup in a hour or so. The captain said it's 4:30 right now and we gotta go up to the track where we gotta ketch the train. Now I git kind o' worried 'cause I been listenin' for a train whistle. All the trains I ever saw blow their whistles one time or 'nother. Only thing is right now, I ain't hear no train blowin' no whistles yet. I hope the Yankees ain't done away with that train.

The captain put out some scouts to guard for sneaky Yankees. He said we gonna move close, up 'bout a half a mile, to the train track 'cause the train oughta be close to Crawford Junction right now and maybe we kin see it.

We git to marchin' the same way we done when we left outta Milledgeville. Me and Billy and two more was the front scouts again. The captain told us to look hard for some place near the train tracks with a flag stickin' up outta the dirt. The flag gonna have a number *one* wrote on it and our train gonna have a flag too, flyin' outta the window of the engine, and it sposed to have a *one* on it too.

Billy git us headin' north and said we sposed not to stumble when we run up on the tracks 'cause it make a lot o' noise. The moon 'bout was gone down in the west now but on the east side, the sun come risin' up. I yell at Billy that I seen a big flag. He come over and he said I was right and I done a good job. We spread out and head on up a ways and wadn't long before, lo and behold, we run right up on two rails.

Billy run back to tell Gunny and the whole bunch of us let out some loud yells. I was happy 'cause we didn't have to walk no more; least not till we git to wherever it was we was goin' to fight them Yankees.

The captain look east and then west down the tracks and git kind o' mad 'cause ain't no train here yet. He probly wonder was we at the right place. I was too. Wadn't no doubt we was at Crawford Junction, so captain said don't worry 'cause it ain't even five o'clock yet.

The captain git everybody to fan out both ways to see kin we find somebody and if we hear a train, come runnin' back. Gunny set me and Billy up in 'nuther patrol to to go straight ahead and see kin we find somebody or somethin' strange and if we find somethin' or somebody, come runnin' back. Fast.

We head north in a near run 'cause we seen how scared the captain was. Billy said if we done a good job, the captain might like us more. The sun git high up and we could see a long way now. We stop and listen and didn't hear nothin' so we kep' on goin'. Then we come to this stream. Well, it coulda been a stream. It was big as a river. We didn't know what to do. We kep' on arguin' 'bout maybe we oughta go cross and keep goin', or split up and check both ways.

End up, it wadn't no problem. Way off to the west we seen a train puffin' up the tracks. He begin slowin' down. We stoop behind some bushes and wait. I 'bout croaked when I saw that train actual had a flag stickin' outta his window. Billy said to run fast as I could and get all the boys up here in a hurry.

I run so hard I fell down two times. But the captain had a fit and fell in it too when I told him what we found. He plain look me straight in the face and said, "Boy, you done another good job. Tell Gunny to get the company on the train. Another company of boys are already on board because they're going the same place as we are. They git on board in Alabama and I don't want a bit of fighting amongst you. Tell Gunny to load from the front because those Alabama boys loaded from the back." So I run off to find Gunny and told him all I could 'member 'bout what the captain said. Gunny give me a pat and said, "Thanks, Homer. You done nuther good job."

'Fore ten minutes was up, all us boys begin findin' seats in the front of that train and it was puffin' along. I was happy and I kep' thinkin' how nice I done somethin' else good 'cause the captain said so. All the time I live 'round Dodgetown, I never had no idea was I gonna 'mount to nothin' more'n a corn grower. Maybe I still ain't, but least now I'm better off'n I used to be.

It wadn't no time till every blessed one o' our boys was sound asleep like a bear in a cave. And not none of them, 'cept maybe the captain, had no idea where we was headed. I begin thinkin' 'bout us boys again and wonderin' how many is gonna come back. And how many ain't comin' back. Pretty soon, my eyes begin to lay heavy and try to go shut. My mind did too. Main thing is, I ain't never been on no train 'fore and I didn't wanna miss nothin' 'bout what a train look like. Might be only time I ever gonna ride one. I gotta 'member every little bit of bein' on the train so I kin tell the folks back home.

I reckon I didn't know when, but my mind musta went goofy and sleepyland come closer and closer over me. When them train wheels begin slappin' tracks, ain't nobody kin stave off sleep.

Musta been eleven or little after, a graycoat I ain't never seen 'fore come through the train tellin' all us they got some food near 'bout ready and to git ourselves up so they kin pass out some. I thought 'bout bein' hungry and 'membered one o' them food bags from Sparta still restin' in my back pack. I opened my back pack and smelt of 'em. Yep, it done spoil now and I chuck 'em out the door to the animals 'long the railroad.

The graycoat, jus' like he promised, and two of his boys, come by and begin passin' out new paper sacks. They was loaded with chicken, potato salad, and some great big biscuits, just like the ones Ma usta give us every mornin' before we go to work in the field. They was also corn on the cob so tender seem you didn't have to even bite to get some off. They told us to come over to the tea barrels and dip some up in our canteen and find someplace to set and eat this good meal. He said our captain was gonna come over and talk to us in a few minutes.

Yep, the Army food they give us on the train was good. When I join up, them boys back home said I wudn't never git nothin' fittin' to eat. They don't know nothin'.

The captain come around and said we was gonna get *ride-tired* for the next few days. He said we goin' to Augusta, Georgia, then to Columbia, South Carolina. When we leave Columbia, we gonna stop at Hickory Flats, North Carolina and take on water, coal, and food bags.

We gonna leave Hickory Flats and go through some tall mountains and pass through Staunton, Virginia and get off the train at Strasburg, Virginia. Then we gonna join up with the 17th Mississippi Infantry Volunteers near Leesburg and put a stop to them Union boys from crossin' over the Potomac River. If I was to add up all the goin' I ever done in my life, it wouldn't come up nearbout far as we been jus' on this trip.

I was terrible sleepy. My eyes shut and I didn't know nothin' for a hour or two. When the train git nearbouts to Augusta, somebody said look outside the window 'cause in a few minutes we was gonna be at the edge of Carolina and we wudn't see Georgia for a long time. That wadn't the half of it. Some of us boys wadn't never gonna see Georgia again.

My eyes was shut but my mind kep' thinkin'. I begin to secret ask God how come wars was. All us boys is really young boys and most of us ain't git married yet. Lotta us won't never get to do their duty in life, like havin' kids to keep the world goin'. I know I ain't never done my duty with no girl yet 'cause the Bible say first I gotta take a girl to a church, stand in front of a preacher, lay my hand on the Bible, give up all them other girls, and then me and her gotta join up like husband and wife do. Then I kin do my duty with her and have some kids. And afterw, I can't never do that with no other girl. I thank God He save me from doin' that when we was in Sparta.

The train git slower and slower, blow a whistle, shot some steam out, and come to a stop. Gunny said, "Everybody gather 'round and quit talkin'. We jus' stopped in Augusta, Georgia and we gonna be here 'bout a hour. They gonna bring us some more food bags, so if you hungry, git one. You kin go outside and walk 'round in plain sight of the train, but you gotta come back quick. If you wander off and miss the train, you in double serious trouble. Means you done gone 'stray from the Army and ain't no officer or no NCO gonna be happy with you at your trial.

"Five minutes before the train sposed to leave, it gonna toot three times. Then a few minutes later he gonna toot one time. That means he movin' and you better be on board. Any questions?

"I ain't hear no questions, so you kin take a quick walk and look around. When you climb back on, git your food bag, and go set down. If you don't set down you might get sick."

I went outside and look under that train and I seen some big pieces o' iron and boards and chains and I cudn't never figure out how any man never had 'nuff sense to make a train. I knowed one thing, I was gonna write Pa and Lotta and Lack a letter 'bout what a train look like at the bottom.

The whistle on that train blow three times and everybody started gittin' in line and pickin' up a food bag and climbin' on board. I git mine and walk toward the middle and set down on a seat. I set in the middle 'cause most of them boys up in the front wanna talk a lot 'bout what bad stuff we gonna do to them Yankees. I set 'tween them two companies where it was quiet 'cause I like to think quiet 'bout back home.

The whistle blow again and the train begin jerkin' and we was rollin'. I look out and we was on a bridge over a real big river. Biggest I ever seen. I don't the name of that river but one that big gotta have a big name. I don't know why they don't put a sign on the edge of rivers so folks crossin' over kin know what is the name of it.

I open up my food bag and pull out a nice piece of fried chicken. 'Bout three bites and I dig back in again. My hand wadn't half-way in the bag when this shadow of a little army boy come up and set down side o' me. It was dark and I cudn't see was it Billy or one o' my other friends. He said, "Hey, Homer."

It was so dark I cudn't tell who it was but I knowed his voice, so I said, "Who you, soldier?"

"You know me, Homer. Lack. How come you don't know your own brother who been your blood kin most all my life?"

I 'bout fell flat over. I never figure I was gonna see none o' my family again till I git back outta this war. "Lack. What you doin' way up here? You sposed to be home."

"Yeah, I know."

"Pa know you here?"

"I don't know he do or not. I didn't tell him I was leavin' and I didn't tell Lotta neither. I left out in the night after I put all the leftover grits in the fryin' pan in my sack."

"You dumb as a snake, Lack. You ain't but fourteen. You ain't old 'nuff to be on this Army train. We goin' up north to fight. Don't you have no idea they shoot Rebs?"

"I wanna go fight, too, Homer."

"Lack, Pa always say you ain't got the sense God give a June bug. How you find us here?"

"Pa git your letter. Soon as Lotta come home from school, he made her read it. He told us what you said and I git secret 'cited 'bout fightin' Yankees. I figure out my plan 'bout how I was gonna go up and see you. When the time come, I sneak away and leave Pa and Lotta and high-tail it to Milledgeville. Them army boys say you was headed somewhere' up to where them Yankees was. I begin askin' all 'round everywhere and final foun' this little Reb boy playin' a horn and he told me where you was goin'. So I look in them tents and taken this Reb uniform wadn't nobody wearin' and left out."

"You walk all the way up to Augusta?"

"No. That little horn blower at Milledgeville said y'all was gonna walk 45 miles straight up from Milledgeville to ketch a train. So I high-tail it that way and I kep' goin' 'cause I knowed I was sposed to come to a railroad. I didn't have no idea where I was, so I walk north. I final come up on this train track and I didn't know which way to walk. I 'cided I oughta walk east."

"How far you walk down the track?"

"I don't know, Homer, but I come to a little town. A man told me it was Greensboro. My legs was so tired I cudn't go one step more so I jus' plain laid down in this little barn and went to sleep. Blest Pete, it wadn't long when some train noise wake me up, so I jump up and run over and climb on it and hid. I figure it was your train. I was still tired, so I put on that little Reb uniform and went to sleep again."

"Anybody figure out you wadn't sposed to be here?"

"No. I walk around like I was sposed to be there and I eat one o' them boy's food who was asleep and I went back to sleep. When the train stop at Crawford Junction a whole raft of boys git on."

"That was us git on the train, Lack. By then they musta been over 200 army boys on that train. How in God's name you find me?"

"I kep' walkin' 'round in the train, one way and the next, over and over, and kep' lookin' every which way. Then when we was comin' near to Augusta I nearbout walk straight in to you. I stop and hide and begin follerin' you 'round. I kep' stayin' near to you and hidin' a lot. I figure I was gonna wait till I see you all by yourself."

"How come you come up here anyways, Lack?"

"I ain't got no use for them Yankees, jus' like you ain't. All that stuff they doin' to us Rebs back home, I wanna go with y'all and fight 'em."

"You ain't even got a gun."

"Kin your sergeant get me one?"

"Only way I figure is keep yourself hid. Soon as we git where they is real shootin', some poor soul gonna ketch a bullet and git laid down to the ground. Do and I'll get his gun and load it and git some bullets and give it to you. And don't let it go off accidental. You might kill somebody you don't want to."

"Ain't no other gun 'round here I could have?"

"Yeh, it is Lack. I been carryin' Pa's gun around too. I got it hid in the front train car. I'll git it for you so you won't look nekkid like a jay bird. But don't talk to nobody. Jus' try to keep nobody from seein' you or Pa's gun. OK?"

"Yeh, Homer."

"Listen and do like I say. We both gotta do like I say or we gonna be in a peck o' trouble like you ain't never seen. First thing, you stay real hid. I gonna tell my friend Billy 'bout what you done. Billy, he gonna stay our friend. He real smart. Smarter'n most all the rest us army boys 'cept the captain and the gunny. I'll tell him you kin shoot a gun better'n I even kin. You keep hid right here. I mean hid. Me and Billy gonna keep gettin' you somethin' to eat and tellin' you what goin' on.

"In a few days we gonna git to a little town name o' Strasburg. Thass where we sposed to get off and hunt down Yankees. Soon as the first gun fall on the ground, I gonna git it and bring it to you. If it was even a Yankee or a Reb, I'm gonna reach down and while I'm pickin' up his gun, I'm gonna pick up all the bullets he got left. Then you stay right side o' me all the time we fightin' them Yankees. OK?"

"I hope I ain't did wrong, Homer. I hope you ain't mad."

Chapter 7

"Southern Soldier Boy"

©Captain G.W. Alexander

We done a heap of waitin' since we git to Crawford Junction. Thass where we was sposed to ketch that train to carry us to whip them Yankees. We finally git on the dad gum thing and we was so tired they told us jus' lay down and rest 'cause we still got a long way to go. Blest Pete, they was right. None o' us knowed how long a ride it was gonna be up to Virginia. I been lookin' to ride on a train all my life 'cause I ain't never rode on one. I final was havin' my wish come true and this 'un is a dilly.

I ain't never been to Virginia but I hear lotsa good things 'bout our Revolution boys, the ones actual save us. Folks back home talk all the time 'bout how bad we whip them British and taken our country back, and how they was treatin' us bad.

Them Revolutionary boys fix it so we could go back to doin' things like we sposed to. When they done that, life git a whole heap better. Then we was happy. We wudn't never have to do no more Boston Tea Parties. Yep, I been thinkin' 'bout that war and how mostly our whole country come together and all us done what we oughta do. I come to be real proud.

Well, now we up and git in a new war. We got lotsa Rebel boys on this train and most of 'em had daddies and granddaddies in that Revolutionary War. Us Reb boys who is headin' up to Virginia is soon gonna be fightin' and killin' boys from up North. I been thinkin' 'bout that. Some o' us boys on both sides actual had daddies and granddaddies in that Revolutionary War. We was bloody fightin' them British, side by side, 'longside o' them boys up North. We was all friends then. We was tryin' to save our new country. But now in this different kind o' war, them of us livin' in the South seem to want to grind the Yankees in the dirt and Blest Pete, ain't no question them Yankees wants to do the same to us Rebels.

I hear some boys on the train yellin' 'bout how many Yanks they gonna kill. Way I see it, that ain't Godly thinkin'. We oughta make us up one o' them ball fields, the one like when we was trainin' in Milledgeville, and every time we git a different mind from the Yankees, we jus' reach in and git out some bats and balls and play a game of baseball. Who gits the most runs, win the squabble and all us go back home and see our folks and plant crops and ketch fish till the next squabble come up.

I ain't sure God 'tended young boys like us to die at the young age we in. I know we all scared. The more time we set on this train, high-tailin' it to Virginia, the more all the talkin' dim down and the boys jus' stare down at the floor. Me and Billy was talkin' 'bout the same thing a few days ago. We wondered is God nowadays puttin' his mind on nothin' but wars and stuff while He settin' up there on His throne in Heaven. We begin worryin' 'bout maybe He done forgit us. Maybe He figure wars is right 'cause back in them real old days, when Moses and David and all them others was alive, they was always scrappin' 'bout somethin'. Maybe thass the way it sposed to be, but it don't make me feel no ways better 'cause in justa few days all us boys gonna be smack in the middle of it.

Billy come back to where me and Lack was hidin' and said the train final gonna be stoppin' in a hour and we gonna get off it. I told Lack he gotta keep from doin' any noticeable stuff and to 'member not to let a soul see Pa's gun. Then me and Lack and Billy walk halfway up to the front o' the train and set down 'mongst a whole bunch of our group. Gunny yell for all us to shut up and be quiet 'cause he gonna say somethin'.

"Soldiers. In 'bout ten minutes we gonna be at the train station in Columbia, South Carolina."

"How long we stayin' there, Gunny?"

"Jus' long 'nuff so we can walk over from this train to 'nuther one waitin' on us."

"How come we goin' to a 'nuther train? How come we jus' don't keep on movin'? That way we get after them Yankees faster."

"We got to change 'cause the train wheels on the train we on now is a different size from the train tracks we got to have to go up to Staunton. That mean this train we on now can't drive on them tracks, so we gotta get on a train that can. More questions?"

"Yeh, Gunny. All that kinda strange. Stupid more'n strange. How far to Staunton?"

"Captain said over 350 miles. Gonna take us over ten hours if the Yankees don't stop us. Maybe more. We sposed to stop in Hickory Flats, North Carolina to git supplies and water and stuff. We probly git some food bags, too, if the Yankees ain't done took over the Hickory Flats Plantation. Thass where some ladies sposed to git together and fill up food sacks for all us boys on the train. Any more questions?"

"Yeh, Gunny. What fool made this 'rangement 'bout train tracks?"

"Musta been some fool Yankee up in in Boston or New York. I don't know and it don't matter none. You foller me off this train. March in one long line, right 'hind me. We gonna walk around for a few minutes and stretch our bones and then git on the new train and stat headed north. And if any o' you dumb 'nuff to leave your stuff on this train, you gonna jus' have to git by without it. Understand?"

"Yeh, Gunny. We ready to go git them Yankees."

"Listen up good. I'm gonna say this one more time. I'm gettin' off first and everybody else gonna foller right behind me and don't shove nobody and don't get outta line. And one more thing. I told you them ladies gonna give us another sack of food. Seein' how it's past dinner time right now, and we won't get no more food till we git to Staunton in the mornin', so don't eat what you got left all at once. Save some for supper. This one they givin' us today gotta last you all the way or you be mighty hungry. And I ain't givin' none o' my food to nobody."

I told Lack he better keep his head down and keep Pa's gun stuck down his britches and keep on not talkin' to nobody. 'Bout that time the train made some noises and come to a stop. Gunny open the doorway, stepped down, and all us went in a line behind him, 'round the station for a few minutes. Then we went over to a new nice lookin' train waitin' on us. All us boys said what a pretty red color it was. We git our new food sacks, one at a time.

Gunny blow his whistle and we all git right up on the new train. Lack was right back o' me and I begin to talk fast to him so he wudn't say nothin' stupid. I told him to keep his head down real low and don't say nothin' to nobody. Me and Lack come up to this graycoat and he didn't have no idea he was gittin' cheated when he hand Lack a sack too. We climb up the ladder and spread out to different seats. Boy, this train was real pretty and got plenty of room where we kin spread out and most every boy could get a whole seat.

All us begin eatin' stuff outta our paper sacks. Some o' us from 'round Dodgetown talk 'bout how people in Carolina seem like they make food a little diff'rent way. I told 'em to shut their mouth 'cause it's free and if they was to make too much noise, we might stir up trouble and Lack might be chunked off the train. He ain't no real soldier noway and they might give me one o' them court days like Gunny been talkin' 'bout. Besides, Lack can shoot a gun faster'n any o' them and nobody never saw how he kin knock the eye outta a squirrel at forty yards and if he come with the rest of us, he gonna wipe out Yankees so fast they can't get no chance to shoot us, so shut up. Most o' them boys sit like they froze in a eye-gaze.

Most o' the boys musta like the food 'cause in nuthin' flat every one of us was sound asleep. Some of it mighta been 'cause this train was runnin' real smooth and wadn't bouncin' and not makin' no loud noise. I taken a look over at Lack and he was doin' jus' like he always done at home. He was sleepin' with his mouth wide open. Pa used to tell him it wadn't gonna be no more flies left in Dodgetown 'cause he be done eat 'em all.

I hate Lack was gonna have to go fight the Yankees, but I didn't know no way to fix it. If I was to run him off the train, ain't no tellin' what might 'come of that little fourteen year old boy. He ain't never been by hisself much. Best thing is jus' let him play like he's a Reb and stay 'round us so we can watch after him. Nice part is, Billy and Elliot and Lawrence and James and me, we promise we gonna keep a sharp lookout on him and keep him hid out and teach him what to do when we go fight them Yankees. Can't never tell, he might start gittin' a lot of joy shootin'

Yankees. That be kinda good for our side, but God don't like nobody fightin' no war for the love of it. Only thing is, we gotta find him a gun. If the captain see he ain't got no gun, he gonna be madder'n a wet hen.

Somethin' peculiar is when you wake up and can't tell you been sleepin' or not. That was jus' how I was today. I figure all my friends was 'wake so I look 'round and I ain't seen a single soul 'wake. Them train wheels was still turnin'. I knowed I was homesick 'cause thass how you feel when you been 'way a long time, specially when you don't know if you gonna never git back. And it git worser when you got a little brother follerin' you and he ain't sposed to be there and you scared the captain gonna see him.

They say our train sposed to take on water at Hickory Flats. I didn't know if we done passed it yet and I hoped we ain't, 'cause I wanna see what they talkin' 'bout when a train take on water. Wadn't no big person 'round so I couldn't talk 'bout it, so I jus' lay my head back and drop off to sleep again. Them wheels hittin' on the track put a real spell on me.

It come a loud whistle sound and I wake up and we begin stoppin'. Gunny come by and said we don't need to worry 'bout when was the train gonna stop at Hickory Flats, 'cause we jus' git there. He said we ain't got to worry 'bout no Yankees shootin' at us neither, 'cause they's a big Reb patrol roamin' roun' outside the train and they keepin' 'em away. He ain't seen them food ladies yet but be ready to git off quick if they show up and bring your gun.

I git me a seat up close to the water tower and I seen this big hosepipe thing pointin' down at our steam engine. That hosepipe was big as my leg and 'fore I knowed it, water begin comin' down it and pourin' in this hole back o' where the train driver sets. I wudda never figure how a train big as this'n could never be pushed 'long by water. I bet the gunny don't know neither and I ain't 'bout to ask no more stupid questions so he kin laugh at me again.

'Bout this time, all the water done run out and hosepipe raised up. Gunny said them ladies from Hickory Flats Plantation jus' come over with the food bags and we gotta git lined up over at the door. Corporal Hinson gonna lead us out to the wagon and we gonna git our food bags and hurry back in the door where our guidon is stuck straight up. That was pretty smart. We all done learned how our guidon looks.

I told Lack to get hisself close up behind me and make sure his face is hid good. I told Billy I was gonna look at every one o' them ladies 'cause

I wanna see if that pretty one with the black coat and the white shirt on, the one in Milledgeville they said was Pauline, was still follerin' us. We all git our food bags and git back in our seat faster'n nothin' I ever saw.

I look over at Billy when we was back to the train and he said he ain't seen hide nor hair o' Pauline. I told him I seen two pretty ones but none of them was like Pauline. Maybe our people done caught her and maybe she in jail somewheres or maybe even she git shot 'cause she was a spy.

By this time we load up and ready to go to where we headed to. Gunny said we was gonna stop at Staunton and get some more water and maybe some food if the Yankees ain't stole the women. It somewheres 'round 250 miles. I was plumb tired o' hearin' all them new towns we goin' to. I jus' wanna finish up them Yankees and go home.

My head kinda flop back on the seat and I begin thinkin' 'bout all the stuff done happen. I was proud o' Lack for doin' a real good job hidin' hisself. Soon as I git a chance I'm gonna sit down and write a letter to Pa and Lotta and let 'em know we doin' OK and how good Lack can hide his head and how he learnin' 'bout all this soldierin'. But I ain't gonna tell 'em the captain ain't found out 'bout Lack hidin' out with us.

Chapter 8

"The South"

©John Hill Hewitt

Gunny come runnin' through the train hollerin' stuff like, "How come you knotheads ain't 'wake? We comin' to Staunton. Be up time we stop. We ain't got all day." I jump up and look 'round and Gunny was right; there all them boys was sound 'sleep. Not no single eye was open. Wadn't long till Gunny's git 'em *wake as a snake*. I 'member a crazy man back at Dodgetown used to go 'round sayin' stuff 'bout somebody 'bein' wake as a snake. He said snakes don't sleep none 'cause they don't need no sleep, so they always wake. I ain't never believed that. Me and Pa always usta say everybody gotta sleep some.

Gunny final cool down and set 'bout talkin' to us. "Listen up, Rebs. We comin' in to a train station and we sposed to do jus' like we done when we was at Hickory Flats. You foller right back o' me when I git off the train. Stay in a straight line. We gonna walk 'round and git our legs stretched. Then we gonna find out if them food ladies is here."

All that time Gunny was talkin', I kep' thinkin' 'bout that pretty Pauline lady in Sparta. If I run into her again, I'm gonna say hey and

57

tell her she still pretty as she was in Sparta. But I reckon if she still doin' spy work, Gunny ain't gonna let me talk to her none 'cause I was the one messed up things when we was in Sparta.

We foller Gunny off the train and, jus' like he say, stay right back o' him while we walk 'round a bit. 'Bout that time I git to shiverin', and Billy run over and talk to this train man, "Mister, it git colder'n this?"

"You ain't seen nothin' yet, soldier. It ain't even snowin' yet."

"Snow?" said Billy. "Mister, us boys ain't seen no snow but maybe a time or two in our whole life. I don't know nuthin' 'bout it, 'cept it white."

Elliott seen we was talkin' to somebody 'portant so he come over and stuck his nose in what we was talkin' 'bout. "Gunny, you reckon we gonna git some heavy coats and sweaters when we git up to where the Yankees is? I didn't bring none."

Gunny told all o' us to shut up, so we did. A bunch of us boys begin watchin' the train load up with water again. I looked over at Elliott and yelled at him, "Blest Pete, Elliott. I still say I don't see how no motor run on water. I reckon if it do that, somebody real smart been stayin' up nights thinkin' 'bout things."

Elliott ain't smart as most the rest of us, so he didn't say nothin'. James musta hear us talkin' and yell out from over at the window, "Gunny, how kin this train run on water?"

"You still on that foolishment? I'll tell you boys somethin'. It either run on water or we all be outside pushin'. Or if that don't work, we jus' hike it up on our shoulders and lug it all the way to Strasburg. I don't care. Only thing I know is we gotta be in Strasburg in time to meet Colonel Featherston so we kin go fight them dad blasted Yankees."

"Them trains too heavy to push, Gunny," said Lawrence.

"Like I said. Any which way what works. Now stop all this rattle-talk. Them food ladies is outside. Let's go out 'fore they git froze. Stack your guns and foller me. Do it jus' like lass time. Git off the train in a straight line behind and close up to me and pick up a food bag and then go right back on the train."

I been thinkin' some more 'bout all them food ladies. They give us good stuff in Sparta and Columbia and Hickory Flats, and now same thing up here at Staunton. But they was all different bunches of 'em from a whole buncha places. Jeff Davis musta been passin' the word to 'em while we was comin' up here. God bless them Southern ladies. Only thing, I still ain't seen nothin' more o' that Pauline lady. Maybe if she git caught, she been put on a chain gang somewheres, or shot, or a rope 'round her neck.

It was 'bout ten in the mornin' when we git back on the train with our food bags. We kep' waitin' for the wheels to start turnin'. All us boys musta been gittin' tired o' this train-ridin'. 'Bout everybody was 'sleep again. Billy come back to where we was and wake everybody up.

"Listen up," he said, kinda soundin' like Gunny. "Gunny and me been talkin' with the captain and they up and made me a corporal and actin' platoon sergeant." Billy dilly dally round a little bit and went on, "Reason is, 'cause we soon git where them Yankees is and itta be hard for Gunny to boss the whole company at one time 'cause when we start bein' shot at, itta be hard to see all us boys and them Yankees at one time. So way it is now, Gunny gonna boss me and I'm gonna boss this platoon and thass that."

All the boys stand up and pat Billy on the back.

"Hey, you gonna git you a stripe, Billy."

"Yeh, but they didn't bring no corporal stripes with 'em. Captain say they gonna give it to me later."

"Then how we know you ain't lyin'?" said James. "They oughta make me a corporal. I can shoot near'bout good as you."

"James," said Billy. "We ain't got time to be fussin' 'bout this. The captain say I git graded up and all the rest o' you gotta listen up to what I say 'cause if you don't, we might lose the war."

James kep' on bein' upset. "Back when we was shootin', I didn't pour all my powder in them bullet packs down the barrel. I was savin' it case I needed it later. That made you shoot better'n me. Thass how come you git graded up."

"James, you wanna go see the captain right now? We kin git this all settled."

"Not now. I'm gonna wait till we meet up with them Yankees and when I start shootin' more Yanks than you do, we kin tell the captain who best."

"OK, but right now, you listen to me. Right?"

"Jus' right now."

"OK. That settled. Y'all listen. They put a passle o' bullet packs in the train. Every man sposed to git a whole heap o' them and stick 'em in your pockets."

"We gonna practice shootin', Billy?"

"No, Elliott. We headin' up to Strasburg where we might meet up with some Yanks. We sposed to roam 'round up there and try to find the 17th Mississippi."

"We gonna fight them?"

"No. They Rebs. They from Mississippi and gittin' bossed by a real smart man, Colonel Featherston. Thass who we gonna join up with. They got 1500 men. We got 'bout a hundred and that other bunch we been ridin' the train with 'bout the same. That mean we gonna have 1700 men when we go after them Yankees."

"Who we gonna fight?"

"Captain say the 15th Massachusetts Infantry. They come down to Leesburg a few days ago and they roamin' 'round, probly tryin' to see whass goin' on."

James run up to Billy and yell, "Hey, Billy. You ain't doin' your job. Train ain't movin' yet. Reckon it ain't broke down? Must be gittin' close to dinner time."

"Settle down and git some bullet packs in your pocket. I'm goin' up to where the gunny and the captain is and see how come this train ain't movin'. Y'all stay right here till I git back."

All us loaded our pockets with bullet packs and stay right where we was, 'cept some of 'em went sound 'sleep. Some other ones begin talkin' 'bout how come we don't git on up to where we sposed to.

A few minutes later Billy come runnin' back and yellin', "Git them guns loaded! Right now! When them food ladies was bringin' our food bags, they seen some Yankees up the tracks 'bout a half a mile north. They got horses and we gotta go git 'em 'fore they shoot our train. Hurry up! Load them guns and git ready!"

Bullet packs was ripped open and ramrods was jammin' minie balls down the barrels. Not more'n a minute later we was ready and we git off the train.

Billy begin to boss us. "Git in scout formation. Like Gunny told us when we was leavin' Milledgeville. Spread out with two men way ahead on the tracks. Them's front scouts. Then another two people go on each side and in the back. Rest o' y'all is the main body, so git in a line on the tracks. Git ready to blow down some Yanks. But don't shoot at somebody ain't no Yankee. Stay quiet as you can."

Look to me like Billy was doin' a real good job. Hard to tell he ain't never been fightin' no Yankees 'fore. He the smartest one in our group and I'm glad he the leader. Everybody else was follerin' him real good too. They musta 'membered how we done it when we was marchin' 'way from Milledgeville and them scouts was watchin' out for Yankees. Billy run up and stay with them front scouts and we was movin' out real good.

Then we hear Billy talkin' real loud from where he was walkin' with the front scout group. "Spread out in a line. Move fast straightways ahead and keep real quiet. Yanks up ahead. Them ladies seen 'em near the tracks, right side o' the tracks. They real live Yanks. Git ready."

We git to almost runnin' and we hear Billy again. "We nearbouts there now. Slow down so they can't hear you. And all a y'all git ready to shoot. Soon as I say.

"Y'all in the scout group over on the right, move over to the left and join up with the front scout group. NOW! Y'all in the scout group way in the back, come up and join up with the left scout group. NOW!"

Billy was soundin' like he musta went to that army school they call Citadel, but I knowed that wadn't right, 'cause he growed up near where rest o' us live in Dodgetown. And he pick more cotton than I ever done.

Next thing, Billy said, "OK, main group. Git up here and fill in 'round the scouts at the front, but don't git too close to one another."

I looked over next to me and Blest Pete, there was my little brother again. "Lack. What you doin' so close up to here?"

"I'm gonna plug me a Yank, Homer."

"Ain't you got no sense. What you gonna shoot 'em with? You got no army gun."

"Have now. See it? I git it from one o' them soldiers in that other company."

"How come he give it to you?"

"'Cause I swap him Pa's gun. He said it look like the one they got at his home and he wanna shoot Yankees with it. He say itta shoot Army bullets."

Our group kep' on walkin' and Lack was still up close. My heart pump like it ain't never pump and my breathin' was pickin' up speed. I kep' on feelin' my gun and talkin' to it. I ain't never been so scared in all my whole life. I cudn't even remember what my brother's name was no more, and I worry if he was scared as I was while he was walkin' up to fight them Yankees. I knowed I oughta be over right next to him but Billy said don't git too close to one 'nother.

"Circle 'round," yelled Billy. "They right up ahead. Git ready." There they was. I seen 'em way up the tracks. One of 'em look like he was tryin' to find somethin'; maybe his gun. One of 'em was tryin' to put on his britches and another Yank was pickin' up his gun and loadin' it. They wadn't but twenty yards out from the front of us now.

Billy yelled out, "Fire! Let 'em have it." We begin cuttin' down on them Yanks. Look like it wadn't but four of 'em.

Everybody shoot one time and begin reloadin'. I look over and seen Lack, down on his knees, shootin' jus' like he always done when we back home shootin' wild hogs. Billy yell out, "Cease fire. We done got two of 'em. Them other two's got their hands up. Y'all come on up and see what kinda luck we done had."

Them two Yanks we shot was layin' right on the ground. Peaceful like. Look like they been sleepin' a whole year. Them other two was holdin' their hands up in the air. Billy said, "Everybody come over here. See whatta happen when you don't have no guards lookin' out for you."

"Them Yankees musta not saw them food ladies. Reckon did they, Billy?"

"Reckon not. Two o' them ladies said they jus' come right by where the Yanks was sleepin'. Musta not had no guards a'tall. Them ladies was plenty scared so they just kep' on a movin' and told the train man."

"What we gonna do with 'em, Billy?"

"We gonna take 'em back to the train. We probly bury them that's dead. Captain said if we got any live ones left, we sposed to git 'em to Leesburg where Colonel Featherston is. The colonel might wanna talk to 'em.

"Gunny said git them dead ones buried and feed all the prisoners and git 'em tied up tight on the train. And don't do no rough stuff with 'em. They jus' doin' the job their captain give 'em. We movin' out for Strasburg and thass where we gonna see what kinda fighters we done git to be."

"How far is it up there, Billy."

"Gunny said maybe a hundred miles. So y'all git some breathin' time. You gonna need it. No tellin' when we kin git some rest. Be watchful when we git on the way. We gonna be travelin' in a kind of a little valley, so y'all can look out the windows, specially over on the left side and you kin see a whole bunch o' real pretty mountains."

James piped up. "What's special 'bout no mountains."

"James, it's 'bout time you jus' plain shut up," said Elroy. "We all happy we git Billy leadin' us. He done a real good job so far and I'm gonna foller him all the way past Virgina and New York while we send them Yanks squealin'."

I always hate seein' two friends down on one 'nuther, so I said, "All in favor everybody bein' friends, raise your hand." Blest Pete, every one of us boys raise his hand up high.

I guess James figure he better straight hisself out with all o' us and he stood up and told all o' us he wadn't gonna do no more gripin' and Billy doin' a good job. Billy stuck out one hand to James and put the other hand on James' shoulder. "James, if I was to guess, I say we gotta tough fight comin' on for many a day. You and me and all us got to work together."

"OK. I reckon I jus' was too much hopin' I could send a letter back home and tell my family and my friends I was bein' a boss. Now on, Billy, I'm listenin' to what you got to say."

"We gonna all be happy 'bout that. You ask 'bout them mountains. Them's the Shenandoah Mountains. The same ones wrote 'bout in that sad song. Now all us gotta git some sleep and be ready for what waitin' on us."

Chapter 9

"Cheer, Boys, Cheer"

©Anonymous

I done what Billy said and laid down on a train seat. This train got seats different from that other train. These was nice and soft and wadn't long till I was doin' like my mama used to say: *Sleep like a bug in a rug.* With all this scariness goin' on so long and me runnin' kind o' shaky, wadn't hardly no time till I come awake and set straight up on the seat. Bless Pete, I cudn't 'member where I was at. I look all 'round the place where I was standin' and cudn't 'member how come I was where I was at. Out the window I seen a whole bunch o' big high hills. They was mighty pretty. Musta been them they was talkin' 'bout.

My head git clear up and I figure out where I was at and I set down. I 'member Billy told us to look at them mountains, so I look at 'em again. Then it come to my mind we was in a war fightin' some boys who was our brothers jus' a year ago. I git kinda nervous like I was when we was fightin' them poor Yankees this mornin'. They didn't have no chance a'tall 'gainst us. I feel real sorry for them boys. Them mountains is too pretty to have a war goin' on 'round here, and I hate for them two Yankee boys to not never git to see them big tree tops no more.

All matter o' things kep' on swishin' in and outta my head. But don't matter how you think, I kep' on thinkin' over and over 'bout them two Yankee soldiers we shot. None of us know did they have a wife and some little kids. If they got some little kids, them kids won't never see their pa no more. Or them boys' mamas won't git to see her son no more neither. Most people got a mama and a daddy. I reckon they did too. I stop thinkin' 'bout what I was thinkin' 'bout and bowed my head and said a prayer to God tellin' Him don't let none 'o us git bushwhacked like we did them Yankees.

This train trip been too long. We come all the way from Crawford Junction and we done git plain wore out. Some of us boys hopin' all this dumb ridin' 'round gonna be over pretty soon. I don't know nobody don't 'gree with that.

Some us keep worryin' 'bout fightin' in a real war. Way I figure, in a real war, they's a whole lotta people out in them shootin' fields, and half of 'em ain't our friend. Wonder how them big men git a war started? Reckon they jus' share out a bunch a bullets to each side and say *go to it*? Reckon they gonna keep doin' it that way? If they do, Bless Pete, some pore souls gonna git kilt.

Elliot say he git to thinkin' 'bout how come we don't 'cide on two captains and put 'em out on the field. Put one on one side and one th'uther. One by one, them captains choose up people, till they git equal numbers so one side won't have no betterment. Then turn 'em loose and see who win, then go to the next war next year. Billy said he git worried 'cause so far Elliot ain't figure out much 'bout war yet and he hope the rest of us does real soon. I ain't and I know most of us in our bunch ain't neither.

Billy laid down on one o' them train seats nearby to mine. I never thought 'bout it a whole lot, but that boy been busy as a hungry duck chasin' a scared beetle. I guess that how it work when you git to be boss. Me and James talk 'bout it and James say he done change his mind and he don't wanna be a no boss no more. I don't neither.

I told Lack to come up to the seat next to mine. We talk a few minutes 'bout our home and how the folks probly was. "Homer," he said. "You know what?"

"What, Lack?"

65

"One o' them Yanks was mine."

"You shot one of 'em?"

"Yeh, Homer. Reckon they gonna give me a medal?"

"How you know one of 'em is yours?"

"Cause I seen the bullet hit him."

"You didn't neither."

"Did too. I seen it. Reckon I can't prove it, Homer, but I seen it. You 'member back home, I usta tell y'all I can see my bullet when it goes out the gun barrel and see where it hit. I seen that one hit that blue coat mid-belly."

"I don't know 'bout that, Lack, but we gotta git some rest. You stay up here near to me when we git off the train. And don't do nothin' thatta draw no 'tention to your face."

I was half-sleep and laid my head back. Them worries kep' on comin' up 'cause I didn't have no idea what was fixin' to happen next. We due to git to Strasburg in two hours. Some of us was talkin' 'bout them Yankees we shot bein' far south as Staunton, and that mean some o' them might be roamin' 'round up near Strasburg too. Ain't no tellin'. I kep' my head laid back and told God I had to git some sleep and Lack too. I told Him please set us down to sleep fast.

Next thing I knowed, Billy was wakin' us up. "Fifteen minutes to Strasburg," he was yellin'. "Git all your stuff in your bindle. Last thing we need is somebody gittin' off this train and leavin' his gun or some bullets in the seat."

I look over at Lack. "Boy, you keep your head down while we git off. And after, too. I don't want the gunny seein' you on this train, and no ways not the captain neither. Hide yourself till we git over in them woods."

"How 'bout Billy? He know I'm here."

"And if we stay lucky, ain't nobody else gonna know you here where you ain't sposed to be. We done hear all the stuff gunny been sayin'; that stuff 'bout how bad it is when a boy turn and run *'way from a war.* But Bless Pete, this gonna be the first time any folks ever hear of a boy runnin' *to a war,* special when he ain't sposed to. Now git packed up and set down where I kin see you."

The brakes on the train begin to sound out a loud noise and a funny squealin' sound and then it come to a full-blowed stop. Gunny run up to

Billy, "Git your boys ready to git off the train, and when they off, git 'em in formation. When y'all off the train, you and me and the captain gonna have a talk with one 'nuther 'bout what we gonna do next. Make sure all your boys ready to move out instant!"

None of us boys was feelin' like talkin'. I wadn't talkin' much 'cause I was worryin' 'bout was things fixin' to change a heap. I got no idea where we sposed to head next after we git off the train. I wonder was some Yankees still hangin' 'round here, and if they was, I didn't wanta go stickin' up my head so some Yankee, one scared as me, was gonna blow it clean off. I cudn't figure out whichaway I oughta look next when they tell me to git out that door. If I do it the wrong way, I know some Yankee gonna see it and blow it clean off.

I gotta stay livin' cause o' Lack. He don't know nuthin' 'bout takin' care of hisself when Yankees is 'round and special if one of 'em point a gun at his head. He ain't never had nobody pointin' nothin' at his head. We used to point guns at one 'nuther a heap when we was younguns and Pa was out in the field, but we never actual pull no trigger. Right now I begin thinkin' I oughta still be back in Dodgetown where Pa is at. That way none o' us probly wudn't see no Yankees for the whole war.

Billy come back from his meetin' and holler 'bout it was time to pick up our bindles and foller him off the train. He said pick up a food sack 'cause we gonna have a long walk to where we goin'. We was pretty fast gittin' ready and soon all us boys was in formation and our group was standin' way back behind a big bunch of other boys. We figure all of 'em was Rebels 'cause it looked like they was all dressed in the same color clothes as us and they wadn't shootin' at us.

The captain begin yellin' out loud and said we behind a lot of time 'cause of the messin' 'round. He said we was already sposed to be left out and here it is gittin' to be nearly noon, but our colonel said we gotta make it up. A bunch of loud talkin' and yellin' start goin' on by the officers and in a few minutes we was marchin' east, outta Strasburg. We figure we wudn't git to where we was goin' till it was dark.

Billy run 'round, talkin' to us boys while we was marchin' and said we got to march over to this town called Leesburg. Some of us ask him was that where General Lee was born but nobody didn't know. He said he knowed one thing. That was where we was goin'. We sposed to find this Rebel high up man name of Colonel Featherston. He boss of a big bunch of boys he brung from Mississippi. Our little group got only 'bout 200 boys and we sposed to join up with them boys from 17ᵗʰ Mississippi and 18ᵗʰ Mississippi and, countin' us, that gonna be 1700 Reb boys for the colonel to be boss of. So far, nobody don't know how many Yankees is there, but however many it is, we gonna go out and sting-whip every dad gummed one of 'em.

While we was marchin', I begin thinkin' a whole heap 'bout this war. Main thing I don't know is why is we fightin' this war. We gotta load up our guns, raise 'em up, pull a trigger, and do it over and over, all jus' so we can make some poor Yankee boy meet God sooner he sposed to. Me and Billy been havin' the same thoughts. We been talkin' 'bout it a whole heap. Heck, it wadn't but a year ago them Yankee boys was our brothers.

The sun kep' droppin' low in the sky and we didn't know when we was gonna git there. Gunny told us a while ago, case we didn't know, today was Oct 20. The sky kinda gittin' dark and I begin thinkin' 'bout them night time pig shoots we used to have back in Dodgetown 'bout this time of the year. They was plenty fun. I figure all them boys, them ones stayed home and didn't wanna go help us fight the Yanks, they gonna be out huntin' in the middle of the nights these days. Ain't nothin' I rather do than be back there right now.

Then Gunny come runnin' up to Billy and begin fast-talkin' and quick-pointin'. Billy look like he know what the gunny was sayin' and in no time a'tall, he git all us moved up to little over a hunnert yards back of 17ᵗʰ Mississippi. Me and Elliot and the rest of us boys look over to the right side and there was this real big river we was marchin' by. I told Elliot it would be nice to throw a hook in that river 'cause I bet I could ketch a whale.

Gunny come runnin' over again to where we was marchin' and somebody blurted out 'bout we didn't know what was the name of that great big river. Gunny said the Yankees call it the Potomac River. I wish Pa could see it. It was real pretty. Them river banks was 'least a hunnert foot straight up from the water, and ain't no slant in the bank. I git to thinkin' I better not git to lookin' at it too hard and wander off too close to the edge and let some Yankee shoot me and send me straight down to the bottom.

The sun been set a long time and I was gittin' real tired. Gunny musta been too, 'cause he told Billy to find us a campin' place somewhere's close to where we was right now. He said some food bags sposed to be here on a mule wagon and we gotta git rested up so we can go after the Yankees first thing in the mornin'.

Me and Lack set up a tent and git in it. There was still some food in the bags they give us this mornin'. It was 'nuff for both us. Wadn't long till me and Lack and probly all them other boys was 'sleep too. Took me a long time 'cause I 'member Gunny talkin' 'bout us goin' after the Yankees soon's we wake up.

It was sometime in the middle of the night when somethin' hit me smack in the middle of my backside and said "Homer!" real loud. Ain't nobody I ever knowed live up here, 'cept Yanks, and I don't rightly know none o' them.

I set straight up and looked 'round and said, "Whazzat?" Then I said, "Whoozat!" I said them thing's 'cause I didn't know what it was hit me in the back, and who neither.

"Homer. Me. Lack. I wanna know somethin'."

I was gittin' bad scared till I seen it wadn't nobody but jus' Lack. "What you wakin' me up for, Lack? We sposed to be sleepin' so all us boys gonna be ready to beat up on Yankees in the mornin'. You and me, Lack, jus' us two, ourselfs, gotta be ready to do that same thing when we wake up. Now go to sleep, boy."

I laid back down and git to worrin' some more 'bout Lack. That poor boy didn't have no idea what we facin'. Truth be known, I ain't neither. I ain't never been in no war before. Maybe a little one, the one where we killed them two poor Yankee boys who didn't have no sign of a chance.

But I knowed all us boys we got on our side was soon gonna run in the middle of a raft of Yankee boys, and wadn't none of us, or them neither, I reckon, gonna be smilin'. This fight comin' soon was gonna be so bad, nobody 'round Dodgetown wudn't never b'lieve it.

Chapter 10

"Ridin' a Raid"

@Anonymous

Most us boys learnt you can't git no sleep when you in the midst o' battlin' Yankees. Maybe, like Ma usta say, we might git *half a sleep*. But last night, some o' us boys even snore all night long. That was good. Only bad thing, right now it might near five thirty the next mornin' and I'm wide-eyed 'wake, worryin' 'cause we 'bout to go at it again.

Yep, I was right. Wadn't but a few minutes, that little horn blower let out a sound on his horn. He begin runnin' in circles and yellin' at us to git up quick. Gunny come over to Billy and said to git us in formation a hunnert yards back o' them Mississippi boys, and do it right now and don't let nuthin' hold up nobody. Then Gunny said eat up all the food we got left and don't waste none.

Billy taken us right to the spot we was sposed to be and 'fore long we was marchin' right behind them Mississippi Rebs, eatin' what we got left. We ain't hear no shootin' yet, so we figure we ain't run into no Yankees yet. So we kep' on marchin'.

That new day showed itself and the sun was makin' the woods and fields look mighty pretty. Gunny say today is October 21 and that big sun rose up where we could see it. I look and there it was, lookin' like a big 'coon huntin' fire, risin' up over the Potomac River. Elliot claim he seen some brim or somethin' jumpin' outta that water. Billy said we wadn't sposed to be thinkin' 'bout fishin' right now 'cause if we do, them Yankees gonna git the drop on us at the wrong time.

Gunny come runnin' over, said some stuff to Billy, and then run over and talk to some other Rebs. Billy said listen up. "We 'bout near to a place the captain call Ball's Bluff," he said. "We sposed to head over to the left and git ourselves in the middle behind them 17th Mississippi boys. We gonna be somethin' they call *in reserve,* and we gonna stay right behind them boys. What we gonna do is watch and see if the Yankees break through. If they do, we gonna fill up the gap, and make 'em wish they hadn't never thought of it. Check your gun got a bullet in it and you got plenty bullet packs in your pocket. The colonel and his boys hear a bunch of Yankees is up ahead, comin' this way, and we probly gonna have a set-to with 'em 'fore you know what's happenin'."

We git over to where Gunny said for us to be at and we hear our horn blower playin' "Charge." That song mean we sposed to pick up our gun and follow whoever we sposed to follow that day and we knowed that day it was Billy. Billy begin yellin' stuff at us. "Keep movin' over to the left. Line up behind them Mississippi boys; back of 'em 'bout one, maybe two, hunnert yards. Hold them guns up and be ready, but don't shoot till me or the gunny say shoot."

'Bout that time, seem like out o' nowhere, some guns way up ahead begin blarin' real loud. Sound like them pig shoots down in the swamps at home. Beside them gun sounds, they was some other bad soundin' noise bein' made, kinda like some boys yellin', or like somebody was gittin' hurt. Me and Elliot and Lack was close by one 'nother. I told 'em, "Y'all keep lookin' for blue coats. Don't let none o' them sneak up on us."

"Kin I go over where they at and shoot one, Homer?"

"No, Lack. Billy say not to shoot nobody till he say so. Hear what I say? Me and you and Elliot and James and Lawrence sposed not to shoot at nothin' till Billy say we kin. 'Less some Yankee come close and point his gun at us."

I look real hard to see what was goin' on but them big pine trees and all them bushes was in the way. I begin thinkin' we was still a fur piece from the fightin'. I seen that big river over to the right again, but we wadn't close as last time.

Billy yell out, "Move up with me. We gotta git to the front line, wherever it is. Y'all can shoot anytime you want to, but be sure you shoot jus' at blue coats. Lets go!"

I yell at Lack and Elliot, "OK. Lack, you and Elliot. Y'all can shoot good, but don't shoot at nobody that ain't got no blue coat on. Jus' like we was back home, pig shootin', and we was sposed not to shoot no cows."

Pretty soon we was up in line with them Mississippi boys. They was wavin' and hollerin' at us. I still ain't seen no Yankees. Billy yell, "Watch out. Keep lookin' for Yanks. They right up ahead. Captain think they gonna try to break our line and we gotta stop 'em."

I yell to Lack, "OK. You and Elliot keep lookin'." 'Bout time I said that, I seen them Yanks sneakin' through some bramble bushes. Musta been five or six, maybe more behind 'em.

Billy yelled, "Now, Lack. You and Elliot. Cut 'em down when you kin line up a good shot. Be ready."

Elliot and Lack move to little place with dirt piled up with a bunch o' great big rocks scattered 'round. Them Yanks blind if they ain't seen us now. Shoulda been shootin' us like shootin' fish in a barrel. I look at Lack. He was kneelin' down like he used to do in a pig shoot. I seen the smoke come outta his gun and he begin whoopin' and hollerin'. I told both of 'em to quit that whoopin' and hollerin' and git that gun loaded again. Right now. Them blue coats ain't gone home, yet.

"I git one, Homer. I git one! I seen the bullet him 'em."

"I think I git one too, Homer!" said Elliot.

Billy come over and seen we was doin' real good. "Homer," he said. "Elliot and Lack both can shoot extry good. I gotta idea."

"What, Billy?"

"Git a group of our boys bunched up back o' them rocks where Lack and Elliot is. Tell 'em to not do no shootin'. Jus' load guns and pass 'em up to Lack and Elliot fast as they can. When Lack and Elliot shoots, tell 'em to pass them guns back. Rest us gonna load 'em and pass 'em up ready to shoot. We kin git a lot of bullets headed at them Yanks."

Wadn't but a minute, we was passin' loaded guns to Lack and Elliot. Each one would shoot and pass the gun back and git another one, and shoot again, and pass it back. By golly, them two boys was shootin' more'n ten times a minute. It was lot better'n when all us boys was each one shootin' one time in more'n a minute.

Billy let out a big yell, "We gotta git more shots. Make Lawrence a shooter too. Git him up next to Lack and Elliot. Pass him some guns to shoot with too."

Lawrence git in a shootin' spot and git to doin' his shootin' job jus' like Billy told him. Them loaders was havin' a hard time keepin' up. All you see was fast movin' fingers and bullet paper flyin' down on the ground. Seem like Billy figure it jus' right, when he put Lawrence on the line.

Them Yanks quit comin' through the bushes. 'Bout that time, that little horn player begin tootin' another song. Billy yell out, "Retreat. That means we gonna quit shootin' for right now. I better go see the gunny and find out why. We been doin' real good."

Lack begin whoopin' and hollerin'. "I done good, Homer. I git a bunch. Six o' them suckers I figure. Elliot say he git five. Lawrence, how many you git?"

"That's good, Lack. Don't git to thinkin' you too good to git yourself shot. We gotta keep knowin' what we doin' till this whole war is done."

Lack yell again, "Lawrence! How many you git? . . . Lawrence, you OK? . . . Lawrence!"

"Homer! Billy! Lawrence layin' on the ground! I think he done git shot!"

Billy come over and look at Lawrence. He laid his hand down on top o' Lawrence head. "Lawrence. He dead. Hit right in the middle o' the neck. I gotta go see Gunny and figure out what we do next."

All us boys flopped down to rest, but we didn't rest none. We mostly talk 'bout poor old Lawrence. We all knowed his pa and ma. All us been fishin' with him. We begin talkin' 'bout what good days we had when we was little.

Billy soon come back. "Eat while we restin'. If you ain't got none, the wagon is back of us. Captain said we done a real good job. Stop the Yankees cold. He said Lawrence done a good job."

"How many we git, Billy?"

"Can't tell, Lack. All he know is eighteen o' them suckers was shot down right out in front of us. Musta been our platoon mostly done it. Captain said he proud but don't let down none."

"I git six, Billy," said Lack. "I seen my bullets hit 'em. I wanta git some scalps and take 'em home so everybody back home see we done our job."

"We don't do nuthin' like that Lack. We don't take no scalps."

"How come? I ain't gonna like it if I can't git no scalps, Billy."

"We ain't Indians, Lack. We don't git no scalps. You gotta 'member that. We done run them Yankees back 'cross the river, but Colonel Featherston figure they ain't gonna give up easy. They shot some cannons from 'cross the river when we was fightin' and they probly gonna try to git 'em 'over on this side 'fore they do somethin' else. Way it looks, we gonna be in a real fight come late afternoon. Now eat some chow and git some rest. Still a heap o' Yanks up ahead."

Gunny run up and git Billy off to the side. They talk 'bout two or three minutes and the captain come walkin' up. We all jump up and salute. Gunny yelled out, "You don't sposed to salute no officer on no battlefield. All them Yanks 'round us kin see. Salutin' tell 'em which one to shoot at.

"I got one thing to say 'fore the captain say his piece. All the fightin' we done was good. We can't forgit Lawrence none, but don't let it heave you none neither. We gotta keep fightin' hard.

"Billy done a real good job when he put Elliot and Lack on the shootin' line. He seen it done such a good job, he put Lawrence up there. Best we can tell, Lawrence git three Yanks. Bad part of it, the Yanks git Lawrence. Y'all be quiet a minute for Lawrence 'fore the captain speak."

Some real still silence come over our little group. I told God how come Lawrence turn up shot dead and rest o' us is safe.

The captain begin talkin' to Gunny, and we was listenin'. "Gunny, I came over to tell Billy that he and his squad shot down maybe a dozen and a half Yanks in that skirmish. I am proud of you. I've never seen a maneuver like that, Billy. I don't know how you came up with that idea but we'll use it again. Colonel Featherston agrees.

"I am sorry Lawrence was killed. We must never forget one of our own. Lawrence is a hero in the Confederate States Army forever. I will be writing a letter to his family.

"In fact, I am proud of all of you. We must have some real good-shooting soldiers in Platoon 151. Keep it up men. We might have some medals to pass out soon. Back to you, Gunny."

"Thank you, suh. We gonna keep doin' our job."

The captain left and we all set back down and talk some more 'bout poor Laurence. We figure we wadn't gonna have no long wait to fight again, so we kep' waitin' for Gunny or Billy to tell us when. Poor Lawrence.

Gunny git me and Billy and Lack to set down in a little bunch. He begin sayin' stuff real serious like. "Billy, any strays in your squad?"

"Strays, Gunny?"

"Yes. Strays. A soldier who ain't no real soldier."

Billy kinda couldn't hardly talk none, but final come up with, "Yeh, Gunny. We actual do. This one right here. Lack. He Homer's brother. Homer join up down in Macon. Then a month later, Lack 'cided he was gonna go find his brother and help him fight. He foller and come across our train close to Augusta and we been hidin' him."

"You oughta done sent him home."

"Wouldn't go 'less Homer went too. And he ain't got good sense. The Yankees wudda git 'im cold."

"How come he didn't just go to Macon and join up and find us up here?"

"'Cause he ain't old 'nuff, Gunny."

"How old you, Lack?"

"Gunny. I be fifteen November comin'."

"You jus' fourteen? What in the name o' God make you come up here and git in all this fightin' for?"

"Got to help Homer, Gunny."

"How he doin' on the line, Billy?"

"Shot more'n anybody else. Shot six of 'em in that last fight a few minutes ago." Billy told Gunny 'bout them changin' how they was fightin' and 'bout loadin' guns and passin' 'em up.

Lack chime in, "Gunny, I kin see my bullet go outta my gun and I kin see it when it hit. And wherebout it hit. I don't never pay no 'ttention to no sights. I jus' raise the gun up and shoot. I kin shoot a fast flyin' pottage nine times outta ten, any day. Jus' like them pig shoots at night back home."

"Lack, you wanna join up?"

"Yeh, Gunny. I wanna be like Homer. I gotta stay close to my brother. I gotta help him git home. I don't wanna go home 'less Homer do too. 'Sides, I wanna git some more Yanks 'cause a Lawrence."

The gunny look real hard 'cross the river for a minute. "Billy, don't none of us say nothin' for a while 'bout this. Leave the boy with Homer. We can't turn him loose for the Yanks to kill. Soon be fifteen. On the line at fourteen. I gotta talk to the captain and see what he say. I hope we ain't all in trouble."

"Right, Gunny."

"Stay close to 'im. Don't let nothin' happen to 'im. See can he actual take care of hisself. After I talk to the captain, I'll git back. Keep 'im safe. His family know he here?"

"No, Gunny. I been thinkin' 'bout how much they worryin', not knowin' where he gone off to."

"They gotta be."

"Gunny, what we got goin' on with the Yanks up front?"

"Them Yankees who come cross the river this mornin' was from Massachusetts. Seem they don't know much 'bout fightin'. Lots of 'em roamin' around out there and we don't figure none of 'em got no plan. They shot some big guns at us but didn't hit nuthin'."

"Gunny, you right what you said. Way them Yankees scrap us them first two times, they ain't got no experience or no trainin' neither. They come 'cross the river and seem not to have no thought what they was gonna do when they git here."

"Billy, jus' keep your boys ready to go any minute. Be sure they git some rest. If I git them Yanks figure out, they gonna hit us again, maybe 'fore nighttime. And with a bunch more people. I'm goin' to see the captain right now. We gotta work out this thing with Lack. Past noon time, now."

"Right, Gunny."

Chapter 11

"All Quiet Along the Potomac"

©Ethel Lynn Eliot Beers

I was glad when the gunny tell us to lay down and rest. I ain't been so dad blamed tired my whole life. If I wadn't so scared the Lord was listenin', I wudda jus' plain cuss.

Somethin' else make me glad. I was glad the gunny final know 'bout Lack bein' here and ought not to be. Nuther thing I been worried 'bout: Is Lack gonna git in trouble jus' 'cause he come along to help me fight Yanks. Wadn't Lack's fault no big army person didn't know nuthin' 'bout it. Blest Pete, I liable to be in trouble too. The boy ain't never raise his hand like us boys done in Macon when we 'greed we gonna fight for the South. And I was hopin' the rest of them boys wadn't gonna git in trouble neither jus' 'cause they know 'bout it.

The gunny say he gonna see will they jus' let the boy join up right now and make him a real Reb soldier. Bless Pete, he been doin' real good shootin'. Only thing be, he ain't but fourteen.

Ain't nobody think Lack oughta be in this war. Me neither. He oughta be back home helpin' Pa do things like milkin' the old cow, fixin' fences, and shockin' corn. Already middle o' October now and time to git corn shocked up. Maybe Lack oughta be in them pig shoots too. I could stand a slab o' bacon from one o' them wild hogs.

Worser, the boy ain't but fifteen. Well, soon be fifteen. And he already done been in two fightin' go-'rounds. Did good, too. Done kill eight Yankees. Two in one fight and git six on the next one. *Kill?* Bible say we ought not to be killin' nobody. Reckon Lack never read much o' the Bible, special the part 'bout not killin' nobody? I ain't sure Lack kin read 'nuff to read the Bible. Ma usta tell us the Bible is powerful readin'. I guess I better have a little talk with Billy about what God say 'bout killin', even in a war. Right now!

I reached over and hit Billy on the shoulder. "Hey, Billy, I don't wanna stop you from sleepin', but . . . ."

"You done done it, Homer. What you want? This 'bout Lack?"

"Yeh. I gotta take Lack over by the river and talk to the boy. But I wanna find out what you say first."

"Somethin' wrong?"

"Kinda. He done shot eight Yankees dead. I been thinkin' when he do somethin' like that, he oughta kinda feel sorry a little bit. But he don't. He whoops it up and hollers ever' time."

"I know what you talkin' 'bout, Homer. It ain't sposed to be no celebratin' thing. Special when them boys in the blue coats is really our brothers and cousins."

"You right, Billy, but . . ."

"Thing is, Homer, God don't want no killin' a'tall, but maybe war a little different. I ain't never hear God say 'nuthin 'bout that."

"Well He 'llowed lot of it in the Bible. I jus' don't like it when the boy goes to whoopin' and hollerin' like killin' somebody bein' the best thing he ever done."

"Go talk to the boy, Homer. We be here a while, I reckon; least till them Yanks 'cide is they gonna come back."

I roll over where Lack was. "Hey boy, you doze off?"

"You sound like Pa, Homer. I'm layin' here thinkin' 'bout next time we fightin'. I'm thinkin' kin I line up two Yanks and git 'em with jus' one bullet?"

"Let's me and you walk over to the river and see can we spot some fish. Ain't far."

"OK, Homer, but it worry me you soundin' like the way Pa used to talk when he done git upset with me."

"Naw, I ain't upset. I jus' wanna talk some. Here. Sit down on the edge 'o this river bank. Ain't it pretty water?"

"Look jus' like back home, Homer. 'Member some o' them days we had right after supper? We usta go down and set by the creek and ketch a mess o' brim. Then we clean 'em and give 'em to Ma. Next mornin', we git up and she done fried 'em crispy and sittin' 'side a big pot o' yellow grits to eat 'em with."

"Yeh, Lack. We gonna be back to them days soon when all this killin' is done finish with."

"When you think we go home, Homer?"

"Soon's the killin' stops. What you think 'bout killin' people, Lack? Think 'bout poor Lawrence."

"Yeh, but our side ain't the one wrong. I don't see nothin' bad with killin' if they the one done wrong. Like when David kill Goliath. Jus' up and done it. That the same, ain't it?"

"Lack, you think God settin' up there in Heaven, lookin' down and havin' a big time watchin' us do what we doin', like killin' our brothers? You think he done picked out which side gonna win the war, jus' like we do when we doin' them shootin' games in Dodgetown?"

"I hope he cheerin' us up."

"They some parts in the Bible where it say it ain't sposed to be *no* killin'. What you think that mean, Lack?"

"You gittin' worse'n Pa when he git after me, Homer. I ain't near got no idea what you tryin' to say. You jus' doin' like Pa usta do."

"Only thing I kin say, Lack, is any day a war starts, and me and you ain't the one in blame o' startin' it, God gonna be understanding when we git our guns loaded case them on the other side come by and try to kill us. We gotta take care o' our kin and don't let nobody kill 'em."

"Ain't that what Moses done a lot; and David; and all them other ones who is thinkin' like we do?"

"Maybe, Lack, but one thing diff'rent. All this whoopin' and hollerin'. I bet Moses didn't do no whoopin' and hollerin' and wallowin' in the mud jus' 'cause them 'Gyptains git drownded in that river. And I bet David didn't do no whoopin' and hollerin' and gloatin' just 'cause that big Goliath giant caught a rock 'side o' his head. If they hadda done it,

God mighta look at how they was actin' and figure he wudn't gonna help 'em no more."

"You reckon he was thinkin' that when I was whoopin' and hollerin' 'bout killin' a Yankee?"

"Mighta been. I can't think like the Lord. None o' us kin. He the only one think right all the time. Somethin' else, Lack. All them boys we shot today probly got daddies and mamas and brothers and sisters. Some of 'em might be daddies and got little babies at home. And them killed today was our brothers a year ago, and we woulda been happy to go on a pig shoot with 'em. Jus' turn out they was born up North."

"Reckon you right, Homer. I ain't gonna do no more whoopin' and hollerin' next time when I bust a Yankee right in the middle of his big fat Yankee belly."

"Lack, I reckon I didn't make no sense to you, but think 'bout the stuff I said. I wonder what Pa and them is thinkin' 'bout you right now. He probly think you wonderin 'round and not know 'where you stayin' next. Time we better git back to where Billy is and see when we goin' some other place."

I laid down and the warmin' sun was makin' me feel good. Pa always was happy with a warmin' sun. 'Bout that time, the gunny come over and git me and Billy in a group and we begin talkin'. "The captain gittin' worried 'bout Lack bein' jus' fourteen. Wouldn't o' been bad if he ain't never been put on the line with a gun in his hand. But now, he done killed some people."

"Whatta happen, Gunny?"

"Homer, the captain headed right now to find Colonel Featherston and talk 'bout it. And you know 'bout that colonel. He follow rules like they was Bible Commandments and he don't like nobody who don't."

"What we sposed to do while we waitin'?"

"Billy, only thing I know is we jus' do like we woulda did if it wadn't no problem. Lack done been fightin' now."

"OK, Gunny. Is them Yanks gonna come back at us soon?"

"You right, Billy. They ain't givin' up. I ain't sure when the captain gonna git back from the colonel's camp, so if the Yanks attack us, set up jus' like y'all done this mornin'."

Billy raise up from where he was settin'. "OK, Gunny. I be gittin' my boys together and recollect 'em 'xactly what we done this mornin' so we kin do it some more."

In a few minutes, Billy put us to practicin' the way to pass the gun and load 'em fast. We talk 'bout what happen when a soldier git shot and who gonna take his place. James still gonna be the man to keep runnin' to git more bullets so we don't run out. I was sposed to set in the back of the boys and kep' tellin' everybody what to do and make sure everythin' runnin' right. Billy say I gotta keep doin' that.

It was gittin' kinda fun. Billy kep' on sayin' we was doin' good and we learnin' stuff better and better. Then we hear the horn blower playin "Charge" and we knowed it was time and Billy remind us to think hard 'bout what was comin'.

We git in our spot but so far ain't no Yanks show up yet. Lack and Elliot git the guns pointed the same way the Yanks come in this mornin'. Ain't nobody taken over for poor old Lawrence yet. Billy musta not thought of it, 'cause he halfway over to where Gunny sets, tryin' to git our 'structions. The rest of us was settin' down in front, ready and able and itchin' to reload them bullet packs. We gonna show them Yanks somethin'.

Then one o' the most dangblasted loudest noise I ever hear in my whole life come thunderin' over us from where them Yankees sposed to be at. But it wadn't thunder. I ain't never hear no thunder loud as that.

Gunny yell out, "Cannons. Watch out. They probly gonna come bustin' through them bushes. Shoot the people runnin' the cannons." I ain't seen no cannons yet. I ain't never seen no cannon a'tall.

I yell out to Billy what was a cannon. He said, "I don't know. Must be somethin' big. Keep your eye open for somethin' big."

Lack and Elliot yell out, "Here come somethin' big! We shootin'." They was right.

I yell out loud, "Loaders, git ready to load guns."

Elliot yell out he seen a great big brass-lookin' gun. One bigger'n a man. Gunny come runnin' over and holler they got a cannon out front of us.

Then we seen it. Boy, was it big. They was some wheels on it and some bluecoats was pullin' and pushin' it toward where we was.

"Shooters, shoot them men pullin' the cannon. Loaders git ready." Billy was doin' things jus' like he oughta. Lack and Elliot let go with two bullets, reach back and git two more guns, and let off two more shots.

Looked like to me we wadn't gonna hold 'em off, so I yell to Billy, "Lemme git up on the line. Gonna need ever' bit o' what we kin do to hold 'em off."

"OK, Homer. You the bes' shooter we got. Git on the line. Shoot straight."

I look to the front and seen we done put down four Yanks with jus' four shots and our boys was sightin' down them barrels, ready to shoot again. I grab my gun and jump up to the right of Elliot and look at what they was doin'. Two more shots go out and one more Yank go down.

I fire off my gun and a Yank went down. Boy, final we was winnin'! Gunny seen it too and he come over and git a gun from a loader and shot a Yank all by hisself and begin reloadin' it. "Good job, boys," he yell. "Look! Bluecoats is runnin'. They done left that cannon and runnin' away. They goin' towards the river."

Them Mississippians begin shoutin' and screamin' and musta git up a whole batch of energy 'cause they kep' shootin' and whoopin'. A few minutes went by and wadn't nobody a'tall shootin' at us.

Billy yelled out, "Charge" and all us boys, Mississippians too, begin runnin' after the Yanks like a hound dog chasin' a fat rabbit. Chills was trackin' up and down my back like it ain't never done in my life. We was chasin' and shootin' at them bluecoats so hard they begin slidin' down them high cliff banks right down to the Potomac, tryin' to git away. I knowed some o' them poor boys must be gittin' drowned in that cold water.

We stop runnin' when we git to them straight-up cliffs and look down. The water was plain full o' blue jackets. I thought maybe some o' them Yanks done git away, but them poor blue coat boys left on the field was 'tween dead and hurt and I told Billy we better git back and see can we tend to 'em.

We pick up lotsa boys that git kilt. What a sad job. Most of 'em was dead. A bunch of 'em was hurt Yanks and a few was Rebs. We taken all of 'em over to the doctor tent. It was gittin' dark and Billy said we gotta see 'bout gittin' our tents up if they been knock down. Me and the rest of the boys eat some rations and laid down on the grass to rest some. Nobody knowed when they gonna hit us again.

Gunny come over and holler at me to git up 'cause the captain was standin' right behind him. He said where was Lack and git him up too. It was so hard to 'sleep on that grass it felt like I was growed to it, but I git right on up. Gunny taken us over to a place where nobody was at. I git kinda scared 'cause ain't nobody never acted like this, not even Pa. And ain't no captain I seen never waited in the back o' no gunny.

"Whass wrong, Gunny?"

"Lack. Thass what."

"He do somethin' bad?"

"Most all us done somethin' bad in our life. Lack, he ain't but fourteen, and General Lee made a rule up when Jeff Davis made him charge o' the Army, sayin' ain't nobody less'n seventeen 'llowed to be on the line."

The captain come up and stand 'side o' Gunny. "Homer, Son. You and Lack have done a great job and I'd like to keep you both with us. The problem is Lack is too young and he has already served on the line."

"You gittin' ready to send Lack back home, suh?"

Gunny put one hand on my shoulder and nuther one on Lack's. "Best way I kin tell you, Homer, is me and you and the captain didn't have no idea Lack wadn't old 'nuff to fight. And he done such a good job, me and the captain wanna be sure both o' y'all don't git in no trouble. The war over for y'all. Me and the captain been talkin' 'bout if you and Lack kin jus' head back to where that train is and git on it and head towards home, maybe wouldn't nobody git in trouble."

"Gunny, I ain't for sure where them train tracks is, and the right train neither."

The captain turned and said, "Gunny, I am issuing an official order for you to take Lack and Homer to Leesburg immediately. Find the right train and be sure they get on it. I'll give you a list of the train stations that'll they will take. I assume they can find their way to their destination."

"Ain't that a little hard on them boys, sir?"

"Maybe not, Gunny. Rather, I call it a one in a thousand chance for us to get ourselves out of grave tribulation and these boys out of here." The captain looked over at me. "Homer, are you two ready to head back to Georgia?"

"Kinda, sir. But I wanna stay here and whip them Yanks."

"We've already whipped them, Homer. They are running north. The war is over for you two. I can tell you right now that a whole lot of Yankees are heading back to where they came from, as fast as they can."

"We beat 'em, sir?"

"Sort of. And you and Lack were significant in this victory."

"I don't have no idea what all them big words is, but I can't wait to git home and tell everybody me and Lack won the war."

"I'll arrange for some medals for you. One day I'll come to Dodgetown and meet with your family and friends. But don't say anything to anybody about this until I get there. I'll bring the gunny and Billy and we'll have a parade."

Lack begin whoopin' and hollerin' and yellin' 'bout me and him was heroes. Least, till the gunny whomped him on the head and told him to shut up and don't ruin it.

"Hey, Gunny," said Lack. "Kin I do a shootin' show after the parade stops? I wanna show them folks back home how good we kin shoot a gun. I want 'em to see how we won it."

"Yeh, sure, Lack. Sure."

The captain told the gunny to git his bindle ready and leave out with me and Lack soon as possible. He told Gunny to see kin he git me and Lack headed toward Georgia, any way he kin. He was bein' so nice and told Gunny to go to the food wagon and git both us some of them new food bags. If any more wars come up and the captain is in charge, I wanna be on his side.

I didn't have no idea how long 'fore we was gonna knock on Pa's door, but I knowed he was gonna be proud me and Lack won the war. He gonna be extry proud when he hear 'bout we gonna have a parade and a shootin' show. Lotta be proud too. That war was strange. Didn't hardly take no long time to whip them Yanks and I reckon from now on, they gonna think two times 'bout messin' with us boys down South.

Chapter 12

"Good Ol' Rebel Soldier"

@Major Innes Randolph, CSA

I was favorable pleased the captain made Gunny take me and Lack to the train station. Ain't no way we wudda figure how to find a train to take us back to Georgia. That captain a mighty nice man and it ain't no wonder the South win the war so fast. Me and Lack couldn't a figure out what direction to go in if we didn't have somebody smart like the captain to start us off.

We git on the trail and the gunny say we been walkin' 'bout three hours and soon we gonna be over to Leesburg where we git off that train when we was goin' over to fight them Yankees. But we gonna have to wait till we find a train goin' south. Pa gonna be singin' *'Mazin' Grace* when we walk up in the yard we tell him me and Lack was the main one who win the war. Me and Lack was mostly pleased it didn't take no lotta time a'tall to show them Yanks what was what.

I been thinkin' what that parade in Dodgetown gonna be like. I think itta be good. The bes' part gonna be when them people 'round home see the captain give me and Lack some medals. I wonder what color they gonna be. I hope mine got a lot o' red in it. Then when the parade over, me and Lack gonna make Pa proud when we shoot real good in the shootin' show. Best part o' this whole thing is, all them people watchin' is ones me and Lack knowed all my life.

I was dead tired when we come walkin' in to Leesburg. Seem like all I been doin' in the army is walkin'. I ain't been a Reb a long time and I don't know how many miles I done walk. When me and Lack git home, I'm gonna tell Pa me and Lack can't work for a day to two so kin we lay down and rest. Good ol' Pa. He likely say we kin.

Gunny told us to wait on the spot we standin' on till he go see when the right train was comin' by. "Lack," I said. "When we git back, you gonna git yourself a job in town, or you gonna work on Pa's farm?"

"I can't do nuthin' but farmin' stuff. I can't drive no train. Fact be, I can't actual do much a nuthin'. Cudn't even when I was workin' on Pa's farm. I wish I could work on some o' them bridges, but I ain't gonna be first one to cross it till somebody else try it out first. Maybe I could be one o' them boys who paint stores in Dodgetown when they git dirty. I can do that. ALL you gotta do in dip in a brush and slap on what color they tell you it sposed to be. I reckon they tell you that."

"I know that, Lack. Poor old Pa ain't had no good crops in better'n five years. Even if we was to have a good crop, old man Hopkins over to the bank gonna come and take what little money we git 'cause we owe it. Don't seem like the Lusta family gonna never git ahead. 'Cept us. Least in the army, we didn't have nobody pesterin' us all the time 'bout givin' back some we owe 'em."

Gunny come back to where we was standin'. "OK, Homer. In 'bout a hour, they got a train comin' through and goin' south. I sign up for a government ticket for both y'all. All you gotta do is give the train man this letter and when he say to, hop on it. The train people know you sposed to git on it."

"We ain't got to pay nothin'?"

"Nope. Jus' hop on it. The train gonna head down to Charlotte and then turn straight 'round and come back. So y'all git off at Charlotte. 'Member, Charlotte. Don't sleep through it. Don't head back up this way. Do and the captain ain't gonna have no parade and no shootin' show neither."

"We ain't gonna come back, Gunny. We got to have us a parade and shootin' show. Pa gonna be real proud. I bet we gonna make all the folks 'round home real proud too."

"Now, Homer, you and Lack set down on this bench. Eat that food you git in them food bags 'fore we left. And git off in Charlotte."

"OK, Gunny. We know how to git off a train 'cause we done it a bunch, but I don't know nothin' 'bout how to git a new ticket and find no train goin' nowhere else."

"Y'all jus' have to 'member what we done. Jus' go find somebody look like a big person and tell him. Itta be lot more easy if you do it at night when all them train people tired and sleepy. Tell him you and Lack been sent home 'cause you done so good. Now, I got to git back over to where we was and help the captain clean up."

"Gunny, reckon the captain need us to help 'fore we leave?"

"No. Y'all git on to Georgia. Plenty of us there to clean up the place. Y'all git on the train when it come in and go. Y'all 'titled to it."

"OK, Gunny. Tell them boys we evermore pleased to have every one of 'em help me and Lack win that war. Tell the captain we like all he done. And tell Billy and Elliott and James we glad they was fightin' too and tell 'em all to come to our parade, and they can bring a gun and join up in the shootin' show. I bet Lack gonna win it."

"I do that Homer. So long. You boys 'member what I told you 'bout how to find trains. If you can't find one at first, jus' wait; they always 'nuther one."

I was kinda feelin' sad when the gunny leave us. I ain't never knowed nobody name o' *Gunny* 'fore in my life. "Know what, Lack? We gonna miss him. He kinda like a mama to us. And he never done much bad to nary one o' us."

"Yeah, Homer. I feel gunnysick."

"Gunny sick? Whatzat?"

"Don't you 'member, Homer, when we was on that train headin' up to go fight in the war, you said you was homesick 'cause you miss bein' back home. Well, I'm gunnysick 'cause I miss old Gunny."

"Come on and set down Lack. We gotta wait on a train." The sky really turn dark when the station shut down them lights. "Look Lack, kinda scary dark and lookin' like we better be watchin' out. Might be some stray Yankees settin' waitin' for Rebs."

"Homer, you got a bullet in your gun?"

"Yeh, I ain't been shut o' no bullet since we kill them last Yankees. You 'member them. Them's the one's we got so good at fightin', we plain whip 'em."

"Ain't it a nice feelin', Homer?"

"Yep. And bes' part of it, won't be long we gonna have a parade and a shootin' show. And I can't wait to see the captain when he come to see it."

"Homer, you reckon the captain gonna actual come to Pa's house and come to our parade and all that stuff?"

"He say he was."

"You reckon he might be gonna send the word up to Richmond so maybe General Lee might come down to it too?"

"Might be, Lack. Pa be plenty proud if a real Reb colonel come to see his two boys. And special if they was to have a parade and a shootin' show too. And 'magine if he was to look up and see the real General Lee comin' over to talk to 'im. I can't wait, Lack. I know one thing. We better git to layin' down on them benches so we git some sleep. Gotta long way to go. And we gotta wake up when we git to Charlotte. Then we gotta figure out how to ketch another train goin' the right way."

I laid down on that bench and I cudn't git sleepy. Them bench boards was hard like bricks. I look over at Lack and that boy was plain out snorin'. He always could sleep anywheres and anytime. Lotsa time Pa had to go roust him outta bed when he already done rousted him out a minute ago. So bad sometime, he taken a big stick to git him movin'.

I been thinkin' 'bout that parade and the shootin' show. The captain and the gunny, both of 'em talk 'bout it, so I reckon it ain't no lie. And they say the war already done finished, but I seen lotta soldiers hangin' 'round this station. Nobody we seen ain't said nothin' 'bout the Rebs winnin'. Jus' the captain and the gunny said it. I reckon they knowed what they was sayin'.

I hear a loud sound. Yeh, a train was comin' in. "Hey, Lack. Git up. We gotta see is this the right train. Git your bindle and your gun but don't shoot nobody. War's over."

We walk up to where the train stop at and I seen this man lookin' like he was one o' them big men. "Mister, this train goin' down to Charlotte?"

"Sure is, boy. Gonna take eight or nine hours to make it down there, 'less we git hit by some Yankees."

Lack stood up in a great big hurry. "Yankees? I thought we done won the war, mistah. Least our gunny said it. Fact is, me and Homer mostly done it by ourselfs up at Ball's Bluff and we gonna be in a parade and have a shootin' show when we git home."

"Son, I ain't hear that news."

"Maybe the Yanks ain't hear it neither," said Homer, "but we keep watchin' we don't git shot at. You say this train goin' to Charlotte, mistah?"

"Yep, son. We most surely are."

"Mister, my name Homer Lusta and can you look at this letter?" I showed him the note Gunny give me and the big man look at it for a spell. I git up and looked at the man. "He said me and Lack gotta git off at Charlotte."

"Yes, 'cause thass where you gotta change to a train with diff'rent tracks, son."

"Like we done at Columbia when we head north?"

"That's it, son. Gimme that paper and you and your buddy kin git on."

"How long 'fore we leave, Mister?"

"'Bout a half hour, I reckon. But you kin git on now if you wanna. Gonna be a long ride, but the train seats on the train a mite softer than them benches out here."

The man was genteel right. We ain't even half plopped down on the train seat till Lack begin snorin' again like he was before. I jus' set there lookin' at 'im and listenin' at 'im. If I hadda not knowed it was Lack, I would say it was Pa. But Pa back in Dodgetown and ain't never been more'n twenty mile away from it. 'Bout his most funnest times is when he go over to take a visit with some o' the Creek Indians. Pa used to fish real good, but nuthin' like after them Indian boys learned him extry good ways to fish. He didn't bring no more'n half of 'em home. He give 'em to the Indians.

The train begin rollin'. So many bad things goin' on I figure I better see whichaway we actual was headed. I seen this man settin' nearby us. He musta been a *real* big man 'cause he got on a suit and even one o' them neckties. He probably knowed which way we headed. I set down on the seat right kinda near to him.

"Mistah, whichaway this train headed?"

"Hello, son. This train is headed to Charlotte. Is that where you're going?"

"Yessuh. Me and my little brother, Lack. We goin' home."

"Home? Are you on leave? Are you wounded?"

"No, suh. Gunny told me and Lack we done won the war all by ourselves, and when we git home the captain and the gunny gonna come down to Dodgetown and have a parade and a shootin' show. I shot down two Yankees and Lack, he shot down six. The captain told us we the ones really won the war and even General Lee might come and see our parade and shootin' show."

"Where was that battle, son?"

"Ball's Bluff, suh."

"Can you boys really shoot like you said?"

"Yes, suh. We kin prove it any time."

"What else do you boys do?"

"Plow mules. Load hay. Best thing is river boat fishin', day and night."

"Did you say boats?"

"Yes, suh. Boats. We real good. We kin paddle a boat thirty mile any night, and not even miss a breath."

"That's good, son. What's your name?"

"My name Homer Lusta. This'n here my brother. His name Lack."

"I see. When have you boys had a really good meal?"

"We jus' been eatin' stuff they give us in them food bags. Sometime it git to be kinda old and bad tastin'."

"It's late now, Homer. You and Lack get a good sleep tonight. We'll probably get to Charlotte about nine o'clock. Don't you boys get off this train without me. Understand?"

"Yes, suh."

"When the train slows down to stop, meet right here. I'll find you. When we get off the train, we'll go to the haberdashery and I'll buy you some new duds. Then I'll buy you boys the best breakfast you've ever had in your life. How does that sound?"

"Good, suh."

"Now then. You and Lack get some rest. Don't forget. I'll find you right here, when we get to Charlotte. Don't get off without me. This train has plenty of good soft seats. Move around until you find one you like. I'll find you in plenty of time. Don't forget."

Ten minutes later, somethin' jab me in the back real hard and I come to. Real fast. I seen Lack was the one thump me. "Homer. Why that man claim he wanna do somethin' good for us?"

"I got no clear thought on that. Only thing I figure, he likely wanna thank us for winnin' the war."

"Yeh. He was talkin' kinda funny like, like he wadn't rightly persuaded we done won the war. If we ain't the ones won the war, how come Gunny said it?"

"Maybe this man ain't hear 'bout it yet. And maybe we just ain't thinkin' right, Lack. Way I figure, he look jus' like one o' them big men. Least ways, if we stay friends with him, maybe we kin least git him to point us the right train to git on and go to on. Then we kin go see Pa and Lotta and tell 'em they better git ready for a big parade."

"Maybe you right, Homer. I gonna lay here with my eyes shut tight and think 'bout first thing I gonna do soon's we walk in the yard at Pa's house."

Both us musta went in a good sound sleep, 'cause next thing I knowed, Lack begin one o' his loud snorin' spells. I lent over and popped him side the head. He come to and looked all 'round like he didn't know his whereabouts. "Whassa mattuh, Lack," I said. "You don't know wherebouts you at?"

"Ain't no sense fussin' at your little brother, Homer."

"We got to find that big man we seen last night. 'Member, Lack, when we git off this train at Charlotte, he gonna meet us and buy us some new outfits. Then he gonna take us to a café and git us a good breakfast."

"I don't see him nowhere, Homer."

"Yeh, he was settin' right there last night."

"Reckon some other Reb done come 'long and go with him?"

"Best thing we can do, Lack, is track him down, like when we used to look for a wild pig we kill and cudn't find."

We walk one way for a spell and then come back the other way. I ain't got no idea when the train was sposed to stop. Least it was rollin' south.

All this lookin' and we ain't seen that big man nowhere. We ain't got no idea what is his name. That wadn't smart. I kep' hopin' to find him quick 'cause I was plenty hungry and me and Lack didn't have no money to buy none and didn't have no way to make no money neither. I kep' hopin' maybe some Reb captain might come by soon and see us in our

Reb suits so we kin tell him 'bout our gunny sendin' us out of the war but we ain't got no money to git nowhere and kin he help us. Truth be, we ain't seen a dad gummed soul.

All this stuff goin' on gittin' me nervouser and nervouser and makin' me more scareder ever' minute. This rackitty train bumpin' down the track make my mind go 'round in a circle. I don't want Lack knowin' how jumpy I was gittin'. He jus' my little brother and I always done best by him. When Ma was close to dyin' and Pa was terrible sick, I give word to Ma I was gonna take care of Lack, and Lotta too, and Bless Pete, I gonna do it or die tryin'. I gotta find that big man. Gotta find 'im.

Chapter 13

"When this Cruel War is Over"

@Charles Carrol Sawyer

I musta done some real pleasin' sleep 'cause I wake up not tired no more. Lack, he jus' his natural self, still sleepin' like a baby. Bless Pete, that boy can stay sleep anytime you don't wake him up. I hope that big man last night 'tend what he say.

This train we on all of a sudden start to goin' slow like it gonna stop real soon. I set up and looked one way and the nuther. I seen a sign with writin' lookin' like it might be *Charlotte* wrote on it. Up near to where I think we sposed to git off, I seen a bunch of people, standin' round kinda like they was gonna git on it soon as we stop.

I lean over and punch Lack. "Git up boy. I think we in Charlotte. Reckon you and me gotta do it all by ourselfs. I don't see that big man."

"Do what, Homer? What we gonna do by ourselfs?"

"I don't that big man nowheres, so maybe we gotta find out how to git on a train goin' to Crawford Junction."

One o' them train men come by and told me and Lack somethin' 'bout this the end of the line. I reckon that mean we gotta git off now.

When we was gittin' off, I ask the train man if he ain't seen a growed up man in a nice white shirt with a tie 'round his neck and some kinda swanky pants and some shoes lookin' like slippers.

"No, son. We don't git many fancy dressers. You lookin' for somebody like that?"

"Yes, suh."

"What's his name?"

"I don't know, suh, but jus' last night he said he gonna find us this mornin' and buy us some breakfast. I need some. Ain't eat for half a day. Both us. Been a long time. And we gotta find out how can we find the right train to go to Crawford Junction."

"I keep my eyes open, son. Y'all have to git off here. Go talk to that ticket man in the office. Maybe he can help you git where you goin'."

Me and Lack walk to where some people was stirrin' 'round. "Lack, keep your eyes wide open so we kin find that big man. If he ain't nowhere 'round, we got to try to find that ticket office the train man told us 'bout."

"Homer, look over there. Is that the big man?"

"No, he got nice clothes but he don't look nothin' like our big man. He too tall."

"How 'bout that one?"

"Can't be him, Lack. He too fat. His belly look like he been eatin' greasy ham and biscuits and finishin' off with banana puddin' for two month straight. Maybe three. Set your mind to 'memberin' what he look like when we was talkin' to him last night."

"Homer, look over there on that bench where the people is waitin'. The one readin' that paper. Ain't that him. That gotta be him."

"Can't tell much. He got that paper too close up to his nose. Can't figure is his eyes closed or is he lookin' at us or even somebody else."

"Yeh. Thing is, he jus' settin' there right now. Homer. If he ain't blind, he oughta be seein' us without no problem."

"You right. Whole dad gummed thing kinda scary. Lack, lets try somethin' and see is it him. Don't look at him no more. Keep lookin' straight at them words on the train. Don't look at nuthin' else, even if some pretty lady come by. Not nuthin' but them words."

"How come we doin' this stuff, Homer?"

"We gonna try somethin'. We gonna see if he think we don't see him, is he gonna come over and talk. We gotta make him think we ain't lookin' for nobody. That way he might come talk to me and you first."

"Homer, I ain't got no idea why we doin' all this, but I do whatever you say. 'Cept I'm ready to set down and eat some grits and eggs all stirred up together."

"Keep your eyes pointed 'way from that big man and keep lookin' right at that train. Maybe we kin see don't he still want to feed us."

"Homer, he comin' over yet?"

"No. Hush up and keep lookin' at the words on the train."

Little while later I seen that big man raise up off his seat and walk 'round a little. He still wearin' them nice clothes. I git kinda scared when he wander over close to where we was. First thing I knowed, he pat my back and said, "Homer. That you?"

"Yes, suh. I know you. 'Cep' not your name. Me and Lack been waitin' 'round to see you, 'cause you told us you might git us some breakfast."

"I'm glad I found you. It's nice to see you again."

Lack come over. "Mistah, we didn't know if you was gonna come back to see us."

"I assure you, I am serious about what I said last night."

"We seen somebody looked like you settin' on there on that bench over yonder, but we was scared he might not be you."

"As I told you last night, our first chore this morning will be to get you some clothes. Are we still in agreement, Homer?"

"Yessuh. Only question me and Lack got is we don't even know your name and we don't know what to call you."

"Let's walk over to a haberdashery while we talk. My name is Edward. You may call me Edward or Ed. My home is a small town in Virginia but because my business takes me to a lot of places, I don't go home often. Does that answer your question?"

"Yes suh."

"Remember, I said you both may call me Edward, or Ed. When we met yesterday, I wondered if you boys would like to come and spend a little time at one of my businesses and see what I do. Would you?"

"Yes suh. Er, Yes, Ed."

"It's difficult to find good young men nowadays, like you boys. If I hire one, the army drafts him to duty and I have to train another one. But you boys have already served your time. Haven't you?"

"Yes suh. Gunny, he told us we done won the war and we sposed to go on home."

In a minute, we come up next to a store with a big glass wall where you could look in without not goin' inside first. I punch Lack and point at all them new clothes.

They was so many nice shirts. And pants. Some o' them pants had belts sewed in on the top. We wouldn't need to buy no belt.

"Mr. Crawford. This store the one you gonna git me and Lack some clothes in?"

"This is it. And remember what I said. Don't call me *mister*. Call me *Ed*."

"Hard to call a growed up man with his first name. Way I think, if we can call you Ed, but maybe it gonna take time to stop sayin' suh."

"That's OK. You boys grew up right and the army continued. I understand. Call me as you like, but if you come to work with me, you may change as you wish. Understand?"

"Yes suh, Ed. What kinda work we gonna do?"

"Let's get you some clothes and a good breakfast and get ready to get on a train that will take us to the town where my office is and you can see firsthand what you and I will be doing."

Me and Lack went in that store and both us begin breathin' hard. I ain't never seen clothes so pretty like them was. Lack kep wantin' one o' everythin' in that there store but Ed said we can jus' git what we need right now.

I final lent over and said to Lack, "Boy, back yonder a few minutes ago, you was sayin' you cudn't wait no more to git some o' that good food down you 'cause you so hungry. We gonna be happy Ed done give us what he done give us, so stop now. Longer you beg and look 'round, longer 'fore we eat."

"Homer," Ed said, "I can't say I blame Lack. War is terrible. We'll talk about that later. Let's go eat breakfast."

We eat like a mama hog. Ed kep' on tellin' me not to bother the boy. I watch Lack and he pile on and eat two plates worth o' grits. Then he switch over to eggs and bacon. I kep' hopin' wadn't too long 'fore we git on the train 'cause I wadn't gonna be able to haul him up the train steps with him so full o' food.

Ed final told Lack he cudn't eat no more 'cause, do, he gonna git sick. And 'sides o' that, we gotta ketch the train at ten thirty. *Ten thirty*, I begin thinkin', *I ain't never seen no human bein' still eatin' at ten thirty in the mornin'*.

All three us begin walkin' to them benches at the station where people wait at and Ed went over to the ticket man. In a few minutes he come back and give me and Lack both a ticket. Wish I cudda watch how he git 'em so I can know how to do it next time. We set down on a bench and Lack said he done eat too much and he didn't feel too good. I told him he better not throw up 'cause food cost lot of money and it might go all over your new clothes and Ed wudn't like nothin' like that.

This little train come rollin' up to where we was and stop. "Right on time," Ed said. "Ten thirty on the dot. Gentlemen, get aboard." 'Bout the same minute we sit down in our seat, that dad blasted train started up again and in no time we was movin' down the track, leavin' Charlotte. I cudn't figure why wadn't no waitin' and waitin'.

We climb up in that train and Ed taken us to the back to a train car where they was four doors and he point at one of 'em. "Gentlemen, that is your room. Look at the number on the door. It is number three. They call it a sleeper car and this is where you will sleep or rest. There are two beds in there. You lie down in those beds and get some sleep. My car is number two but I'll be going up to the front of the train for a while.

"We'll be going through Spartanburg, Greensville and then stop in Gainesville, Georgia. We don't have to change trains any more. It's about two hundred miles and, if we have no problems, we should get there about four or five this afternoon. When we get there, you gentlemen will learn what happens in my business. You will have an opportunity to decide whether you want to join me and make more money than you ever could make in the army, or probably anyplace else."

A few minutes later, Lack said, "He gone, Homer. What done happen to us? We ain't never had no chance like this."

"You right, Lack. Look at them beds. They soft like a feather pillar. He talkin' 'bout we could make a bunch of money. 'Stead o' goin' back to help Pa farm, maybe we oughta make a lotta money with Ed and send Pa bunch of it. And it sound like that stuff he sayin' gotta be true or he wudn't say 'less it wadn't true."

"Think we oughta tell him we done made up our mind?"

"No, Lack. Lets see 'fore we tell the man."

Chapter 14

"Flight of Doodles"

@Anonymous

I hear that new friend we got, Ed, talkin' real loud. Fact is, he was yellin' out loud, sayin', "Get up, Homer. You boys can't stay in those nice warm bunks all day. Our train is coming in to town and I'm guessing this will be your new home. Get up and let's go see it."

"What the name of it?"

With all that talkin' and squealin' goin' on, Lack come wide awake and begin settin' straight up in his feather-soft bed.

"What's the name of this town, you ask? Like I told you, our train just pulled into the station at the beautiful and peaceful little Southern town of Gainesville, Georgia."

"This where your business be, Ed?"

"Sure is, Lack. If all goes well, meaning you like me and I like you, you and Homer will be very happy here."

"What we gonna do here?"

"Gentlemen, you are precisely what I need in my business. You have the chance to work with me and learn my supply and transportation business."

"What kinda work we gonna do, Ed?"

"What kind of work? Here is an example. Your pa is a farmer. He probably grows several crops. Among them is one that comes to my mind: corn. He grows corn. Am I right?"

"Yes, suh. Thass mostly the mostest one he grow."

"How many bushels does your pa pick in a year, Homer?"

"Ain't a whole heap. He only plant 'bout five acres. We ain't got 'nuff people to do no more. Pull thirty bushel a acre."

"That's a hundred and fifty bushels. Now, what if he could pick five or six thousand bushels in a year?"

"Most gonna go to rot, Ed. Pa can't pick no five thousand bushels in a year. Ain't got 'nuff people to pull it."

"How much corn do you actually use?"

"Pa and us in the house, we eat a bunch of roast' neers, maybe ten a day. We got a old cow and some mules and they eat a bunch. Then me and Homer always takes a heap out to the grinder. First, I shuck some and Homer turn the handle. Then we switch 'round. When we finish, we sack it up. We put grits in grits bags and the rest in meal bags and hang 'it in the smokehouse so the weevils won't get in it. Then we take what all's left to the corn crib. If it set too long a while, rats ruin it in no time a'tall."

"And most of the corn the rats ruin makes your pa really riled up. In this business you're getting in, you don't have to worry about weevils and rats. You'll get paid for your work. Nothing goes to rot. You'll learn all about how to ship our products to far away places so your work brings in money."

"Ship corn? How you gonna do that? Ain't no boats in Dodgetown. Jus' fishin' boats."

"It's getting late. We're all tired from our trip. We'll talk about it in the morning. Right now, I'm taking you to the boarding house and getting you a room. The lady at the boarding house will feed you all meals while you're in town and you'll never be hungry."

"How we gonna pay the lady?"

"You don't. You work with me in my business and I cover all your expenses."

"Ed. Why you bein' so kind with me and Lack?"

"Just as I said. You help me in my work and do your job and I'll handle your needs. I want good men. In addition to your clothes, your food, and your lodging, I'll give both of you ten dollars a week, every week you work. You can spend it any way you want."

"We kin do that, Ed."

"Then come with me. Let's go over to Mrs. Wilkes boarding house and see about getting your room. I'll meet you there at seven in the morning and we'll go to my office. That's when we can talk about what could be your next job?"

"We be ready, Ed."

I cudn't believe me and Lack got us a room in the upstairs with two real good beds. Both us git a whole bed. And lotta room. Lack and mine's was all way cross the room from one 'nother. Even git a bath room down the hall with a thing to pee in. Back home we git three beds in one little bitty room and we can't hardly squeeze by to go out in the yard to pee.

Somethin' really please me is the food Mrs. Wilkes spread on the table for me and Lack. It was fried chicken and mashed potatoes and sliced 'matoes and some great big biscuits, good as any I ever eat. And Blest Pete, she give us a great big glass o' sweet tea. Then she done went too far after we got done eatin' our supper and she give each one a saucer full o' peach pie. She a nice lady too, 'cause she say she be hope she see us three time every day and we gonna like it here.

Me and Lack cudn't hardly go to sleep for thinkin' 'bout all this good luck done come to us. Them beds so soft I set down on one and 'bout git lost. We ain't never had nobody kindly treat us like Ed done, 'cept maybe them boys we run into when they was buildin' that railroad 'tween Milledgeville and Sparta.

Me and Lack kep' talkin' 'bout how God musta actual had a strong notion 'bout Ed and shine a bright light right down on him. I hope one day He gonna think 'bout me like that too, 'cause I wanna go to Heaven and meet all them friends o' mine; them that git that same light shinin' on them too. I hope we kin meet up and start up a baseball game and have fun playin' till we can't move.

Final, I told Lack he kin go ahead and keep on talkin' all he want to, but I was too tired to hear nothin' else he say. I reckon he didn't pay me no mind 'cause last thing I hear was him still talkin'. I ain't got no sense o' when he shut up, but Mrs. Wilkes come by and knock hard at our door. "Boys, it six o'clock. Time for breakfast. Ed say he comin' by in a hour."

"Yes, maam."

"Now, I know you ain't nuthin' but boys, but I wanna hep you git 'long good with that new boss you got. Go down at the end of the hall and you find a room that got a washin' tub."

"Yes, maam."

"Git a bath and it ain't gonna cost nothin' extry. Dry yourselfs off and put on some o' them clothes Mr. Ed bought you. I'm gonna cook you some grits and ham and eggs and biscuit. Itta be ready in no time a'tall. Ed, he gonna come by to git you at seven o'clock. I want you boys to be good workers for him. Y'all hear me?"

"Yes, maam. We gonna do it."

We run down to the end of the hall and open the door. Blest Pete, I seen one of them bathin' tubs settin' on four legs.

"Reckon how we make water come out, Lack? Reckon we pull this little ring?" I was right. When I give it a pull, water come gooshin' out and wadn't no time that tub was full 'nuff for a whole bunch of people to git in. Me and Lack climb in and git some brown soap and we begin rubbin' it all over. It feel so good I coulda kep' on washin' for hours, but I knowed Mrs. Wilkes wudda jumped all over us.

We dry off and git on them new clothes and 'fore you know it, we was settin' down at the table. Mrs. Wilkes look us all over and pat us and said, "You boys know how to wash good. Now you fill up them plates and lemme know somethin' else you might like."

Wadn't nothin' better'n that food. Me and Lack eat a fill and Mrs. Wilkes said it was 'bout time for Ed to show up. 'Bout time she said it, here he come in. "You boys ready?"

"Yes suh, Ed."

"I see Mrs. Wilkes got you full and you got the right clothes on. You ready to go?"

"Yes, suh."

So me and Lack and Ed tramp 'cross the street to a big brown buildin' made outta rocks, and it had a sign say *Watkins Supply* on the side. It only taken a minute to git there from Mrs. Wilkes place 'cause it was jus' 'cross the road over near a big tree thicket. Ed git out a key and unlock the door and we go in. I wudda thought a buildin' old and racketdy like this'n might smell to high heaven, but funny thing, it smell jus' like the fresh of a spring mornin'.

"You boys look around," Ed said. "I have to check on a couple of things in my office. Won't be but a few minutes." We seen some mule wagons and lotta sizes o' big wood boxes and a few little biddy boxes and some long, thin boxes and lotta things I can't hardly 'member. I seen army tents and horse saddles and even some o' them fishin' boats you paddle with. All I was thinkin', was this gonna be fun if we kin do a good job and help Ed sell all this kinda stuff we seein'.

"Whatcha think 'bout all this, Lack?"

"I ain't got no evermore idea 'bout how to use none of this stuff. I hope he don't tell me to fix somethin' he got that git broke."

Then I look over in another little room layin' off to the side and they was some more o' them same big square boxes I begin wonderin' why they was so many. Then they was lotsa things I cudn't figure out what none of that was, so I jus' up and quit tryin'. All this was strange and 'citin' too. When I seen all this stuff, I begin actual knowin' this was gonna be the best job in the world for me. Lack, he don't know what to think, 'cept he ready to work here too 'cause I said it first. I gonna write a letter and tell Pa and Lotta 'bout our new job and we be workin' with stuff we got no knowin' 'bout.

"Homer, you reckon Ed gonna look 'round and find stuff broke and make us fix it? I might take some o' this stuff and give it to Pa. Special somethin' that done git broke and we can't fix it. Pa kin fix anything."

"I reckon so, but I betcha he gonna tell you and me to fix somethin' ourselfs. Maybe that gonna mainly be our job."

"I don't know neither, but Blest Pete, we gonna try. A real good man like Ed ain't gonna tell you to do somethin' you ain't got 'nuff sense to do. Special if you ain't been learned how yet. You 'member that now and evermore, Amen."

Ed come back in. "Well, boys, have you looked around?"

"Yes, suh. All this stuff is 'citin'. We gonna be doin' stuff with them boats and wagons and stuff?"

"You boys will be working with just about everything in here."

"We gonna be fixin' boats and things?"

"Sure. And a few more things, too."

"We kin fix boats. Pa had a old boat on our farm in Dodgetown. We used to put in at a bend in the Altamaha River to go fishin' and huntin'. We bring home lotsa fish. We gonna fish some?"

"Oh, the good old Altamaha. It's one of the finest rivers I've ever traveled. Fish? Sure. We'll try to find time to fish."

"We gonna drive some boats?"

"Lots of them. At times, you might be cruising very close to the place near your home. How far down the Altamaha have you traveled?"

"Went a lotsa times. Most time we git jus' where we was aimin' to go. Bunch o' people up our way go to big pig shoots way down the river. We go to 'em too and always come back with 'nuff ham and bacon and jowls to last us a year."

"You find your way back by yourslves?"

"Yes, suh. I don't 'member no time we ever git lost. We showed a heap o' lost people how to git back home when they was lost. When we done that, they sometime give us a slab o' bacon."

"Seems like you boys know how to get out of trouble when you get in it."

"Yes, suh. Maybe one day kin we go see Pa and Lotta when we nearby."

"Maybe so. When you get accustomed to what we do and if we have time. At first you'll be busy learning and practicing. We'll be busy, but just hold your horses. The time will come."

"Ed, we gonna haul corn and stuff in them boats in that room?"

"If you notice, boys, those boats are probably larger than any you've ever run. Some of those paddles are bigger than paddles you've used. They are oars. Then over here, you'll notice that we also have normal size paddles."

"Look like runnin' them boats take a man with real strong arms."

"That's why, Homer, that most of the time when a boat takes out its load, two men will be riding in the boat. The one in the front of the boat doesn't try to power the boat. He uses his strength and paddles to guide it. The rear man is responsible for powering the craft."

"Me and Homer gonna be ridin' in the same boat?"

"Yes. At least, until you learn two things. First, you have to learn to control those big boats. Second, you have to learn every mile of our river routes. Then we'll be mixing teams."

"Kin we git in a boat and git goin'?"

"Patience, Lack. Today, I will assign what we call a *boat captain* to you. The three of you will haul a boat to our landing and put it in the water. Then Lack will get in front; Homer in the rear. The boat captain will occupy center seat. Your job is to learn to control the boat. And you must remember that the boat captain is always in command until you are assigned a run. You obey his orders."

"We ain't gonna take no corn or pigs or nothin'?"

"No cargo during early training trips. After that, the boat captain might even be with you for a while. He'll be training you in hauling cargo. You'll be doing actual, but not extensive runs."

"I think we gonna like this, Ed."

"Good. We'll spend this morning getting a training boat ready. At noon time, you and your boat captain will take your boat out and you'll start learning to handle it. It's a lot bigger than what you're used to. Go over to Mrs. Wilkes at noon and eat lunch. Then, pick up enough food for supper for you both and a ration for your boat captain."

"How long we be gone, Ed?"

"At first, training trips are a few hours. When you finish training, your trips will be three, four, sometimes five days, or even more, Lack. Many trips will be night time. That's the best time to run."

"How come at night?"

"Think about it. Summertime is hot, but it's cooler at night. You probably know that. Have you ever plowed a mule in the field at night?"

"Yes, suh. Run nice and cool at night. I reckon boat be like a mule."

"OK, boys. Time to get down to real business. Now, let's meet Charlie. Charlie, come over here. This is Homer and Lack. They just came in from the walking army and will be working with us, if they can learn and qualify. Your job is to train them to run the rivers, like the Oconee and the Altamaha. You know what you're doing, Charlie, because you've trained many boat crews before. Lack and Homer are familiar with small river boats, but not our bigger boats, nor our specific mission. Shake hands and good luck."

"I be ready, Ed. They look like good boys to me."

"Then, get with it."

"OK, boys," said Charlie, "Let's git started. We gonna git you ready to go no time a'tall. I done picked out the boat we gonna use. Since you done done a smatterin' o' boat work, we gonna use this great big'n. That OK?"

"Yes, suh."

"You boys don't say *suh* to me. Jus' like Ed. My name Charlie and thass whatcha call me. OK?"

"Charlie, this boat look like it gotta dog house settin' in the middle."

"Yep. Thass where you keep your food and rest when it rain and stuff like that. Ed call it a cabin. You boys don't git used to it. You gonna be busy paddlin'."

"Homer, go git three o' them big oars from over to that stack. And git one o' them little paddles too."

"Oars?"

"Thass what Ed call them big paddles. They got a little iron pin. Two o' them oars go up front—one on each side. Stick them little iron pins in this hole in the top rim o' the boat. Them little pins hold the oar down to the boat when you paddlin' and keep it from jumpin' up and down. Now put the other paddle in the back of the boat, same way. You ain't gonna use that little paddle 'cept when you in close places."

"How 'bout this other paddle, Charlie?"

"It's a oar. It go in the back. The man back there use it to steer the boat. The front man make the boat go."

"How come we usin' these great big paddles?"

"Cause when we runnin' in the water, we might come up on somethin' make us have to skidaddle fast. If we only usin' them old paddles, whoever be chasin' us, might ketch us in a minute. Here, let's go out and see what I mean. Y'all grab that there end and push towards me. There. See it. It's goin' in the water."

"Charlie. Where this water come from? Look like it jus' come right up to this buildin' and run right inside. I ain't seen it 'fore right now."

"It do run inside. Pretty soon it git to be part of the Oconee River. Six month ago, Ed git a whole bunch o' mules and dirt pans and we work on that channel for a month. When things git to goin' slow, Ed brung a bunch of slaves in from a man up in Chattanooga. Them boys was used to work and when water was comin' in, they act like they was up in Heaven."

"I ain't never seen nothin' like this, Charlie."

"Yeh. Look down this long channel. Only way you kin see the river is be in it. All them bushes growin' on that bank make it secret. No way people outside kin see in. Now you boys gotta 'member—you can't never tell nobody nothin' 'bout this channel. Know what I'm sayin'?"

"Not never?"

"Not never, 'cause if you do, it jus might be a sad day for you and who you tell. Now git in the boat."

Blest Pete, wadn't but a minute that boat slud right in the water without makin' no noise. Charlie told us to git in. I git in the front and Lack in the back. "Now, don't y'all grab no paddle till I tell you. I want you to see what I been talkin' 'bout. Now lemme show you somethin'."

Charlie jump in that boat and set in the front seat. He grab them two big paddles in his hands and paddle down that channel, goin' straight like a arrow. I cudn't see nothin' from where I was settin'. That channel was dug so good, I cudn't see twenty foot away. Pretty soon, Charlie said, "Hold on, soldier boys. We 'bout to git in full river. Here we go."

Charlie begin paddlin' fast. Them paddles was turnin' so fast they look kinda like them steamboats I seen pitchers of in New Orleans. Water was plain out churnin'. Me and Lack look in wonderment for a while. I reckon Charlie musta git a little tired. I wudda. He kinda slowed down and turn 'round and show us a smile.

"Charlie. You git this boat to goin' like a gator chasin' it. How come Ed know that work like that?"

"He know lots 'bout boats. You gonna find out. You workin' for the best boat man in Dixie. Now we gonna stop me from havin' all this fun and gonna let y'all practice some. 'Member, the front man doin' the power and the back man steerin'."

Me and Lack ain't never had much fun as we did that day. Charlie say it was time to come back in so we kin eat and git some more food to eat when we go back in the boat tonight with him. Then we gonna learn how to run a big boat in the night.

Little more'n two week pass and me and Lack and Charlie was in that boat every day and 'bout every night. Fact is, it done pass in to November. I git proud o' Lack 'cause he was doin' real good, and Charlie say I was too. I knowed that. Then Charlie git me and Lack to run the boat where me and him was the only boys paddlin'. Right when things was goin' good, Charlie always made us quit and change places. I was havin' such good fun, I cudda stayed on the water all day. Lack said he cudda too, mostly 'cause I said it.

One day Charlie say we gonna do somethin' special tonight. "Boys. Tonight we got a long run. You know what that mean?"

"I reckon we gonna take a load o' corn or somethin' to someplace needin' it."

"You 'xactly right, boys. We gonna leave at midnight. Don't have no idea how long we be gone. Mrs. Wilkes gonna have some some food bags. Pick 'em up 'fore you come. One of 'em for me, so git it too. Git here early. We gonna leave on the button at midnight. OK?"

"We be here, Charlie."

"Homer, what you reckon we gonna do?"

"Kinda scaredy. That Ed a likeable man. I think he OK. He ain't up to doin' us no harm, or nothin'. Reckon?"

"Reckon we jus' hafta wait 'round and see. Least we makin' money. More'n we ever had."

A - Dahlonega

B - Gainesville

C - Bishop

Oconee River

Augusta

D - Milledgeville

Macon

E - Dublin

F - Glenwood

Dodgetown

G - Jesup

Altamaha River

H - Darien

Watkins Supply
Route Map

Chapter 15

"Ridin' A Raid"

@Anonymous

"Come on, Lack. Charlie gonna be mad don't we git to work on time. And we still gotta git them food sacks for when we runnin' that boat."

"OK, less go."

We run over real quick to Mrs. Wilkes, and how 'bout that, Mrs. Wilkes done already put food in them sacks. They was lotsa food in 'em this time. She give me and Lack a real good extry sweet cookie, pat us on the back, and told us bye. Lack eat his cookie 'fore we was half cross the street.

"Homer, what we gonna do when we git in them boats? We been runnin' boats a long time but I ain't run no boat big as these is."

"You right, Lack."

"Must be gonna be gone a long spell. You ever saw such a big food sack like we got?"

"No, I ain't. Guess it gonna be a long time. Maybe thass why Charlie goin' with us. Reckon we gonna be gone a long time."

"I be glad to git goin'. I like what we been doin' but I wanna git some money Ed been talkin' 'bout."

"Me too, Lack. Way I see it, Charlie gonna go with us so we kin practice for the actual reason we come here, I reckon. Ain't no way we kin do a whole new job we ain't never done 'fore and don't know what we sposed to do. Charlie gotta show us xactly what we sposed to do."

"Kinda scare me, Homer. Reckon it ain't gonna be so scary 'long as Charlie stay with us. But what we gonna do if he jus' up and quit work."

"I betcha he ain't gonna quit 'cause I reckon Ed pay him a heap every day. Charlie know a bunch 'bout paddlin' boats. And 'bout what we gonna be doin' too. We gotta 'member ever'thing he gonna be learnin' us."

"Well, I been thinkin' somethin'. What Ed mean when he say runnin' boats?"

"We gonna find out tonight."

Me and Lack go in the buildin' and Charlie, he turn 'round and say, "Y'all done good. They's three people and four food bags. Reckon it one extry, jus' in case. It better match up what we gotta have."

"We ready, Charlie."

"OK. Git them oars in the boat. That'n right over there. B-11. B mean the home base for that boat is right here: Gainesville. 'Leven means the boat number. If we was to go down to Milledgeville, all them boat numbers start with a 'D.'"

"Sound like good sense, Charlie."

"We gonna be usin' old number B-11 for the training stuff we do. Go pick up six o' them oars and one o' them short paddles."

"We gonna tote somethin', Charlie?"

"Yep. Wudn't be no sense o' trainin' without nothin' to tote. See them boxes in load stall 'leven? Thass what we gonna load up. All of 'em. Any time we go on a boat run, we carry the stuff in the same load stall as the boat number we in."

"Hey! Who thought that'n up?"

"Yeh. That-a-way, can't make no slip-up."

"Can't never tell with some o' them folks we got workin' 'round here."

"OK, pushers. Put number 'leven in the water and lash it tight to the tie down. We don't want no boat goin' off on a run all by itself."

Me and Lack tow B-11 'round the little channel and lash it to a tie down. Then we go over to stall 'leven. They was three boxes and we begin pickin' 'em up one by one and totin' 'em over to where number 'leven was tied up.

"Charlie, how much them boxes weigh?"

"Not much. 'Bout fifty pound, each one."

"What Ed got in 'em?"

"Jus' might be anything. Lemme make you a hint. Don't never ask no question 'bout what we carryin', 'cause Ed, he gonna tell you when he 'cides you got to know. And not 'head o' time."

"We hired yet, Charlie?"

"I ain't got no idea. I jus' do what he say. And he ain't told me I kin talk 'bout nothin' goin' on here. Y'all got to hear everything from Ed. Git them boxes in the boat and let's git goin'."

So me and Lack lug them three boxes over to B-11. We scatter 'em out in the cabin so all the weight don't go in one place. Thass what Pa used to tell us, but we didn't have no boxes big as them we usin' now. And we didn't have no cabin on our'n. Lack, he run back to git the food bags 'cause if we didn't have 'em, we was gonna be in a passle of hurt.

Charlie come up 'bout that time and say we was doin' a good job gittin' B-11 ready to go, even if we still in need o' trainin'. "This ain't gonna be no special long trip, so we kin git a bite right now if y'all want." This was kind o' Charlie and I knowed I was gonna like workin' here if Ed let us keep on with Charlie.

I eat one o' them ham samages. Lack did too, reckon 'cause I did. Charlie line us up how we sposed to go. He call it *leavin' port*. He say we ain't in the navy, but we gonna call it like navy people call it if they was doin' our job. Charlie point Lack to the front seat and me to the back seat. He set in the cabin door, right close to where them food bags set. 'Bout that time he said somethin' like "Anchors 'way." I didn't have no notion o' what that mean, but he say it mean we was leavin' port. More I saw how Charlie work, seemed like he sooner be in the navy than whatever it is we in.

"Push us off, Homer, and jump in quick. Use that short paddle to git us movin' slow. Slow. Don't make no noise. When we git out o' this channel, turn to port. If you ain't no navy man, *port* mean left. You know your left hand, Lack?"

"I been knowin' my left hand since I first knowed I had one, Charlie."

"OK. Case you ain't been noticin' of it, the end of this channel got what Ed call a *channel marker*. This'n got a big **B** on it. That mean we in Gainesville and we 'bout to leave this channel and go right in a little river we call Oconee Tributary. It 'bout the same as the real Oconee River, but it jus' ain't growed up yet. Then we gonna turn to port. 'Member what that mean?"

"Yeh," yelled Homer. "Turn to port mean left turn."

"Good, Homer. Keep paddlin' with that short paddle and keep quiet."

"How far, Charlie?"

"'Bout a hunnert yards, Lack."

We keep paddlin' so nobody hear nothin' from B-11.

"OK, boys. Look up 'bout ten foot up a big oak tree and you see a **B** sign. Keep on paddlin' with that short paddle like you did them boats you used to do at home. Real soon now, we gonna be goin' out in the edge of the Oconee Trib and turn north. Then we gonna git underway in a natural run. Watch for a **B**."

"Charlie. I hope we kin soak up all this stuff you learnin' us."

"You won't have no trouble. Ed got all our channel spots marked. You kin spot 'em night and day, if you know what to look for."

"I see it, Charlie," said Lack. "There. Right there."

"Good man, Lack. 'Member how it look. Every channel marker we got the same foot high. Ten foot up."

"I gonna turn left. Right, Charlie?"

"No, you gonna turn to port. OK?"

"I call it wrong. We turnin' port right now. OK, Charlie?"

"Yep. Listen. You goin' to Dahlonega. You got 21 mile to go and then you gonna find a channel marker off our port, ten foot high, with **A** on it. Understand? That be Dahlonega and if Sarah be there, she got the bes' food anyplace 'round."

"Yeh. How kin we know when we been 21 mile?"

"Jus' gotta jedge it. Fact be, a usual paddler kin row a boat 'bout three mile in a hour if it ain't no water current pushin' or pullin' them."

"I can't learn all that. You gonna hep us?"

"I won't git you lost. But I might *let you git lost*. I ain't gonna say too much first off. You try it. Now go. We got 21 mile to go with a one mile an hour current facin' us. Means we gonna actual make jus' two mile every hour. Keep that in mind."

"How we gonna know when a hour is over, Charlie?"

"Ed ain't gave you no wrist watch?"

"No."

"Reckon he forgot. Here, use mine till we git back. Strap it on and don't let it drop in the water. This'n cost me a dollar 'cause I had to pay for it. Lost the first one Ed give me. Look at the watch. We ten minute late. Ten minutes past midnight. When we gonna git there, Homer? Keep paddlin' while you figure."

"Charlie, I can't rightly figure."

Lack perk right up. "I know, Charlie. Two mile every hour and 21 mile gonna be little over ten hour to git there. Gonna be after half past ten tomorrow 'fore we pull in."

Charlie give Lack a extry hard look. "Where you come up with that, boy?"

"I always good at figurin' out that kinda number stuff. I always figure Pa's plantin' needs."

"He tellin' the truth, Homer?"

"Yep. Lack always been a good man to have when they was wild pig meat to cut up, fields to lay out, and stuff to buy at the store so old man Johnson won't lie 'bout how much we owe."

"Then let's get ourselfs movin'. What time it now, Homer?"

"All this jawin' 'round, it done git to twenty past midnight, Charlie."

"Then let's get movin'. You boys gonna git us to Marker **A**, on time, without no trouble. I gonna git me a nap. Ed gonna be happy 'bout us havin' you boys 'round."

Chapter 16

"Ridin' A Raid"

@Anonymous

"Come on, Lack. Keep movin'. Paddle hard. Charlie gone to sleep and he ain't woke up a single minute all durin' the night. Least he ain't fussin' at us."

"How long we got to go, Homer? My arms feel like they fixin' to drop off. Ain't used to this. What time it be?"

"Charlie's watch say it fifteen to ten. If what you was sayin' last night when we was startin' off, 'bout gittin' there 10:30 in the mornin' time, we better start lookin' look for that big **A** up in a tree."

"I been lookin' for a hour, Homer, and I ain't seen it yet."

We begin starin' hard up in them trees, wishin' we could find it and final git some rest. I git to worrin' 'bout makin' a fault and gittin' Charlie mad. Then I seen somethin'. Charlie was right. Blest Pete, I seen a big **A** nailed up on the tree 'bout high as one man standin' on top nuther.

"Look, Lack. Over on the left. Reckon I oughta say *over to port.* Up in that magnolia tree. See it. A big **A** stickin' right on the tree. 'Bout ten foot up."

"We done good. Maybe Charlie gonna tell Ed so we kin stay workin' for him."

Charlie come 'wake and listen to what we was sayin'. "I ain't never saw no boys do such a good job as y'all done all night. You boys right. I got to tell Ed 'bout how good you was when we git back. Look under that **A.** Look hard and you kin see a channel o' water. Goin' right through them bushes. See it?"

"Yep, I see it Charlie. Jus' like the one down where we come up from."

"Paddle in and go under that **A.** Do and you be right in the channel. Go slow and be quiet. Lack, you the shooter. Git your gun ready case we git trouble. I got mine ready."

I cudn't figure why we need a gun, but we pull in and paddle slow, tryin' to be real quiet. We kep' on goin'. That channel was so long I worry 'bout fallin' off in some big ravine. Hard to b'lieve, but 'bout time I begin to worry a heap, that channel run right up to a door with a canvas flap over it. We row under that flap like it was a apron, and Blest Pete, we was in a great big room kinda like the one Ed got down in Gainesville. They was more boat docks than Ed got in his buildin', but they look jus' like 'em, so we rowed up to one and tied the rope. Me and Lack was proud to git there 'cause we bless'd tired.

Charlie jump outta the boat and run over and talk to some man standin' next to a door. Little while later, he come back and told me and Lack don't never go in that office door. He said we kin go in a little room right next to it. That got some cots and a big table full o' food Sarah sent over. We kin git a fill o' food and when we git 'nuff to eat, we kin lay down on a cot and go to sleep.

"You boys don't eat too much, cause it might make you sick. I call you when we ready to leave. Gonna maybe be a hour or two so don't git nervous 'bout when. Might be more'n that."

"You want some help movin' them boxes?"

"No. These here men kin do it."

"What we doin' here, Charlie?"

"Ain't I told you? Anythin' Ed want us to know, he tell us. You boys done a real good job so far and don't mess it up gittin' too curious."

"OK, Charlie. I ain't meanin' to git too curious. This jus' real 'citin' work we doin' and my mind git in a knowin' tick. I don't want Ed to git no hate on us."

"OK. Every notion I got say Ed gonna hire you boys permanent. I hope so. I like you boys."

Me and Lack went in that food room and we git a 'sprise. They done brought in some stuff from Sarah. It was fried chicken and mash 'tatoes, collards, corn bread, and a syrup barrel full o' sweet tea. Man, that was good eatin'. I kep' on tellin' Lack don't eat too much. "Lack, if you eat too much and git sick, we ain't gonna git permanent hired. If we don't git permanent hired, Ed gonna fire us. Now quit it."

He quit stuffin' hisself and both us git on a cot and went off to sleep. Wadn't no time Lack was sleep 'cause his snorin' sound go all 'round the room. I cudn't git to sleep 'cause I was thankin' God we git such a good job and gonna be makin' 'nuff money so we kin send some home to Pa. Ma, she gonna know 'bout it first 'cause she in Heaven already, lookin' down at what happenin' right now.

Wadn't long 'fore Charlie was shakin' me and Lack and sayin' time to git up 'cause we goin' back where Ed stay. Charlie whack Lack on the shoulder. "Git up and say hey to this pretty lady. She work over cross the street in that restaurant. She brung us more food bags so we kin eat on way home."

"How do, ma'am. I know it gonna be good. Which'un mine and Lack's."

The lady handed one to Charlie and two to me and Lack. Charlie dig right in and 'bout a minute, it was gone."

"Reckon we can eat and paddle the same time?"

The lady smiled and said, "Yes. You boys probly can. Think about me when you taste this fried chicken." That lady was rightly pretty and I ain't never seen many pretty ladies pretty as her. 'Cept that Pauline lady.

"Lack, old boy, I gonna eat mine now, but I gotta ask you a question."

"Charlie, I hope this'n ain't no harder'n none o' them others."

"Let's see. We come up here twenty-one mile and taken us little over ten hours. Right?"

"Yep."

"How long gonna be to git back?"

"Lemme think 'bout this'n." Lack crook his head and flap his eyes for a minute. "I know this'n, Charlie."

"What is it?"

"That river goin' one mile a hour all by itself. Then we git to figure how fast me and Homer kin paddle without no river. We kin paddle three mile a hour if the river dead still. That mean we gonna go back to Gainesville at four mile a hour, Right, Charlie?"

"You on the money, Lack. So how long it gonna take to git back?"

"Little more'n five hours, Charlie."

By time Lack quit stammerin' and told Charlie, Charlie done ate ever' stick o' fried chicken in his bag. "Bingo, Lack. I can't wait to we git back and tell Ed how good you kin figure. OK, boys. They git B-11 loaded up with boxes. Clock on the wall say time right now is eleven. What time we git home, Lack?"

"Be little past four, Charlie, near time for supper."

"Can't trick you, Lack. God give you somethin' special. Git in the boat so we kin skidaddle."

"We got more boxes goin' back, Charlie?"

"I keep tellin' you boys you ain't got no reason to wonder 'bout things got nothin' to do with you. Ed gonna tell you 'bout stuff on his time."

"OK, Homer. Reckon I forgit too much."

I told Lack to quiet down 'bout things he wonder 'bout 'cause we don't wanna lose this good job. I told 'im this job gonna give Pa and Lotta and us too, good pay like we ain't had in a long time, like not never.

I cudn't figure how come Lack know 'bout comin' up so quick to answer questions 'bout how long to git somewhere's. He always say he don't know why. Jus' come in his mind.

We come rowin' outta that big room with the canvas flap and begin easin' down the channel. We ain't been saw by nobody. Maybe we was stayin' hid from Yankees, maybe jus' plain robbers. I ain't for sure. Maybe it was them Rebs Ed didn't want us to git near to. If we sposed to have some good paydays, I don't care who we sposed to stay way from, that what I gonna do.

We git at the end of that channel and I look up and sure 'enuff, I seen the 'A' up in the tree. I knowed we was headed right. "OK, Lack. We gonna turn starboard, right Charlie?"

"Somethin' I like 'bout you boys. You learnin' good. Starboard it is. I'm gonna lay down in the cabin and rest. You boys wake me up at four 'clock. I wanna have a long talk with Ed."

Charlie claim his belly begin achin' bad so he laid down and snuggled hisself 'mongst the boxes. Reckon he plain eat too much. I look at them boxes and wish I knowed what was in 'em. I knowed I ought not to look in 'em, but I reach down in the box near to me and git to tryin' to lift up

117

the lid. I come close to gittin' it where it might raise up but the dad gum boat run square in a log floatin' maybe a inch under the top of the water. It make a loud wham and Charlie jump up and yell, "Whatzat?"

I said I don't know, but think we hit a log. Right quick I look at that box lid and I seen it was back settin' on the box like I sposed to. Blest Pete, that was close, so I 'cided I jus' gonna keep my hands to myself, my feet, and everythin' else too.

"You boys jus' learnt some extry good trainin'," Charlie said. "Lack, you in the front of the boat, so when it come daylight, look out for floatin' things. One day we even seen a few gators way up here. I gotta lay back down where I was and to git my belly feelin' good. Wake me up at four 'clock."

Lack begin talkin' 'bout how it look like we actual was goin' faster when we go this way. I was kinda gittin' sleepy and I hope I wudn't drop off and Charlie ketch me. I 'minded Lack we gotta keep one 'nuther wake. I reach down in the water and spatter some water on my face. That sleepy kinda went way, so I settle down to be the steerin' man in the back.

Me and Lack was goin' a mighty clip with cold air hittin' us in the face. Git to where it wadn't no trouble to stay wake. I stay high curious 'bout them boxes. Me and Lack both seen them men loadin' 'em. When we load 'em yesterday to come up here, we jus' reach down and pick one up. Today when them men put them boxes in the boat, musta been three or four men pickin' up every box. I can't figure out why me and Lack ain't had no trouble loadin' down at channel B, and it taken three or four men to pick up a single boat up at channel A. Them boxes change how many pounds they weigh? Well, I 'cided I ain't gonna let it worry me none; right now nohow.

Me and Lack begin talkin' 'bout how that river look different from one back home. I ain't seen no fish jump or nothin'. Even if I seen one, I cudn't do nothin' 'bout it. I ain't got no pole or no worms neither. But I still wonder what them boxes got in 'em. Ain't shaped like nothin' I ever seen.

I look over and all o' Charlie's eyes was close tight. "Lack," I said. "You still got a whim to know what in them boxes we can't open?"

"No. Charlie done told us we can't ask no questions 'bout work. Quit worryin' 'bout it. You gonna be like Ma used to tell us 'bout the snoopin' rat. 'Member? He come in our house so much, he forgit they was plenty food outside he could eat, but he want to find out what was in the smokehouse, so one day he go in and Pa shoot 'im dead."

"OK, Lack. Whole thing git me in doubt." So I shut up.

We come runnin' down that river and I knowed we gittin' close to Gainsville 'cause Charlie's watch say it was ten to four. I told Lack watch for that big **B** 'cause Charlie ain't gonna like it if we go sailin' past the channel. "One thing, Lack, I gittin' kinda empty in the belly."

We look real hard and 'bout ten after four when Lack seen it. "Turn in, Homer. I seen the **B**."

We turn to starboard and curve in that channel and begin slowin' way down. Jus' a minute we paddle under that canvas and right up to the place our boat sposed to go.

Ed come out o' the office and wave. "Hey Ed. We done git back. Charlie still sleep. He git sick and say he was gonna sleep and don't git him up till four."

Ed git in the boat and shake Charlie. Charlie ain't moved no muscle. "Homer, when was the last time you talked to Charlie?"

"We bump 'gainst a log after we come outta channel **A**."

"He say anything?"

"No. Jus' said he was tired with a belly ache and keep quiet and don't ask no questions 'bout nothin'."

"Charlie's dead, Homer."

"Dead? Reckon he been runnin' the river too long."

"Poor Charlie. Leaves us kind of slack on people. You think you boys can take over some runs all by yourself?"

"Yeh, Ed. We know jus' what to do."

"It's now past five o'clock. Go eat supper. Mrs. Wilkes has some good eating tonight. Get a night's sleep and be here at eight in the morning after you eat a fine breakfast. We'll talk about what your new job will be. OK?"

"OK, Ed."

Chapter 17

"Oconee Trail"

@Anonymous

"Good morning, boys. It's a sad day. Poor old Charlie. He was a good friend. We'll miss him a lot. God rest his soul. Hope you had good sleep, in spite."

"Yeh, Ed. Charlie a nice man. Both us sad we ain't never gonna see him no more till we git to Heaven. He perfect knowed how to run a boat."

"That leaves us short, but with everything Charlie told me about you, I believe you'll fit in perfectly. You know boats and you know river work. You did it before you got in the army. Are you ready to get to serious with your new army job?"

"We ready, Ed. We wonderin' is we still in the army. Ain't nobody said nothin' 'bout it."

"Sure you're still in the army. Secret army. But I am paying your wage, starting this week. Come with me." Ed taken us in his big office. Charlie told me and Lack since we still in the army, we gotta keep ever'body from doin' wrong. Main thing he said was don't let nobody go in his office but big people. Me and Lack thinkin' maybe we be big people soon.

So much done happen. I git to thinkin' I gotta write a letter to Pa and Lotta and tell 'im me and Lack is kinda big people now and the army still bein' overly good to us.

Ed taken out some maps and stuff and laid 'em on the table. "Here's your next run. It'll be a long one. You're goin' to Station D, Milledgeville, but you can't contact anybody on or near that army base. You are doing secret duty. Secret. Understand?"

"Yeh, Ed. Secret duty. I never figure we was ever gonna do no secret duty."

"Well you are. That's why all of us, every person working for our company, may know only information that he has to know."

"We do that, Ed."

"You'll use B-11 again and leave at noon today. With Charlie gone, you'll be on your own, but I believe you can do it."

"We gotta find 'nuther one o' them channels?"

Ed opened a map. "Yes. Here's where the Oconee goes around the outside of Milledgeville. This map shows two twenty-foot-high granite rocks on the west side of the river. Right here. See? Sticking straight up. Ten feet apart, just north of the bridge."

"I 'member goin' cross that bridge when we was findin' our trainin' field. I ain't seen no big rocks."

"You'll see them. Look for two huge granite rocks. West side of the river. They are there. Right here is the entrance to the channel. The channel marker is a **D** on the top of both those rocks. When you get there, turn to starboard and go between the rocks. Fifteen feet inside the channel, you'll go under a big canvas curtain like the ones you've seen before. Go under it and run about fifty yards. Keep going in that water entrance and into an old building that looks like the one here. Dock your boat and give this envelope to Carl. He's the man in charge.

"Now, boys, on this run you'll be empty going down. Carl will load up your boat with some empty boxes; the same kind you've seen here. When Carl releases you, bring them back here. This is not only a training run, but it's a real run as well. We need boxes back here.

"Now, as to timing. Leave at noon today. The distance is about 110 miles from right here, channel marker **B** to channel marker **D**, in Milledgeville. Do either of you know how long it'll take you to get there?"

"Yep, Ed," said Lack. "Little more'n twenty-seven hours."

"How did you figure that, Lack?"

I 'cided I better tell Ed 'bout Lack and all his knowin' numbers and river speed. He was mightly blowed 'way, specially when Lack told him we was gonna git there the next day close to three in the afternoon.

"You probably won't make it that fast, Lack, but that's good figuring. You can't run hard all night and day. Best thing is when one man gets tired, let him sleep and the other paddles. Then swap out. I'd say you'll get there about six. Carl will be ready. Get some sleep in his cots.

"You'll leave the next morning at four. We seldom run in the daytime past a big town like Milledgeville. It's the state capitol, but especially, an army town."

"That 'cause we secret?"

"Sure. And nobody needs to know our business. Another thing. While you're on the water at night, don't make noise. Same reason. Nobody needs to know our business. You men are more important now than you have ever been. You can do a good job."

Me and Lack left out at noon. I begin wonderin' how come it ain't no marker **C** nowhere. Blest Pete, I learnt the alphabet in school and 'c' come after 'b'. Anyway, I wadn't gonna fuss with Ed none 'bout the way he name stuff.

It turn off cold when it was gittin' dark, but paddlin' help us stay warm. We done a heap o' boat travel at night in our time, so we was feelin' right at home and peaceful. 'Fore long it was breakin' dawn and we git up pretty good speed. Lack figure a half a day to go.

I set to wonderin' what Carl gonna be like. Can't be no better'n Charlie but I ain't gonna tell him I like Charlie best. Poor old Charlie come down powerful sick in a hurry. Scare me.

I begin hopin' they got some good food in Milledgeville so we kin take some good stuff to eat on the way back. Maybe they got 'nuther one o' them real pretty ladies to bring it over, too. That'n Ed had was highly pretty, kinda like Pauline lady in Sparta. I 'member what Gunny say when we was eatin' that food in Sparta. He say all pretty ladies look like one 'nuther. Guess I ain't only one smited over Pauline.

We been movin' right long. Hour ago, I told Lack he need to lay down and sleep long as he want and when he git up, I can sleep. He done that and I git to wishin' some o' them boxes was in the boat. I can't figure no idea how come all this hubbub over jus' plain boxes. Must not be jus' plain boxes.

Lotta deer was comin' down to drink in this river. Ed ain't told me I could shoot one so I figure I better not. Might 'ttract 'ttention from somebody we don't want no 'ttention from. That old sun warm things up and make them leaves on the trees pretty as God wudda want.

"Homer, you still in the boat?"

"Where you think I be?"

"I knowed you was, but I reckon I jus' said it. You wanna git some sleep?"

"Yeh, Lack. I could fall down right now and wake up past Christmas. Wudn't you like to have a old nice Christmas day, Lack? Like when we was all home, and Pa and Ma and you and me was there, and Lotta was a little baby?"

"I think that a lot, Homer."

I sleep a long time. When I wake up I said to Lack was he still in the boat. That was crazy 'cause thass what he said to me when he wake up. I look at old Charlie's watch and it show after five o'clock. "Lack. We somewheres near to Milledgeville. We gotta not say words too loud 'cause Ed say Milledgeville too big a town for us to talk loud in. Gittin' to be kinda dark so we gotta keep our eyes wide."

"I got my eyes strainin', Homer. We ain't gonna miss that **D** mark. First we gotta find them big rocks standin' up in the water."

"Gettin' dark, little brother. Look good."

"Homer. Look way up 'head o' us. Ain't that two big high rocks?"

"Could be, Lack. Keep goin' slow. Time right now ten past six. Run over close to them rocks."

"I see it, Homer. I see a big **D**. We done got here."

"Be real careful. Turn starboard, Lack. Get that gun ready, jus' in case."

We paddle in and Blest Pete, we in the channel in no time. We was goin' slow and seen the canvas door and we run right under it. There was the boat house. Jus' like the one in Gainesville and Dahlonega.

"I don't see nobody, Homer."

"Pull over to the dock so we kin tie up the boat, Lack. Somebody gotta see us and come talk."

Two men come outta a room carryin' guns. "Who you? Don't reach for no guns."

"Mister. I ain't gonna do no shootin'. We lookin' for a man name Carl. See. We in B-11."

"I'm Carl. You got a envelope?"

"Yeh. Ed give it to us."

Carl read the letter. After a few minutes he put his gun away and said, "OK, boys. You done a good job. Right on time. Y'all go in the sleep room and git some good food. After you git all rest up, we gonna git your boat loaded and Ed want you sent back 'bout four. Gonna be a long trip. Over two day."

We go in where them cots was. "Lack, two whole days gonna be a long time."

"Yeh, Homer. 'Cause we goin' upstream."

"Well, better get to sleep."

I reckon we was sleep a long time 'cause Carl start to shake me and sayin' it four o'clock and we gotta git up and git ready to go. We put back on our shoes and eat some o' that food on the table. They done taken all that old food out and changed to some new real good eatin' food.

"Don't stuff your belly, Lack," I said.

"You right," said Carl. "'Member pore old Charlie. Reckon he stuff down too much eatin' and git a bad belly ache. Kinda scary. We ain't never had nuthin' like this 'fore."

"Reckon his food bag git too old?"

"Ain't no way to tell."

'Bout time we git all full up, Carl said this lady name o' Lucille was gonna bring in some food bags that got good fresh eats and it wadn't gonna spoil 'fore we take our run back up to Gainesville. Carl and his men loaded up old B-11 with six heavy boxes.

Lucille come in with them food bags for me and Lack. Yep. Lucille was a pretty'un, too. I seen it even in the dark. Gunny know what he talkin' 'bout when he told us all pretty ladies look same way. When Lucille give me them bags, I look dead at that lady and Blest Pete, I seen the same kinda eyes I usta see on Jeannie, that girl I git crushed on in school, and Pauline, the lady in Sparta in that black coat and a white shirt. Jeannie and Pauline both got brown eyes, but Pauline's more darker. And Pauline got black hair and Jeannie got kinda dark brown hair.

Then I 'cided I better quit thinkin' 'bout pretty ladies 'cause times is it make me lose track o' what I sposed to be doin' and I begin thinkin' 'bout things I got no bizness thinkin' 'bout. This job me and Lack got now ain't no place to lose track of what you sposed to be thinkin' 'bout and thinkin' 'bout what you ain't sposed to. 'Sides, we gotta pay 'ttention to the Word o' God.

Me and Lack pull out to the channel and Charlie's watch show 4:10. We sposed to leave at four but ten minute don't matter. We kin make it up in no time. We git down to the end o' the channel and our eyes wadn't yet matched to the dark. When I say dark, we cudn't see no more'n Saul after God put the blin' on him on that road to somewhere and turn his name to Paul. We run right out 'tween them big high rocks and I say, "Turn port, Lack."

Blest Pete, wadn't long 'fore we git to runnin' nice and a low moon come up behin' and give us 'nuff light to find our way back to Gainesville. Lack say could he sleep a little and I say OK. Every time one us wake up, the other one hop to it. Funny how when I git to runnin' on the water, specially at night, old man Peaceful join up with me. Pa always tell us that God on your shoulder. Well I b'lieve that and I figure I gonna let that old Man ride anywhere He dad gummed well please. Whole world His anyhow. I 'cided to quit thinkin' so we both kin 'joy the ride.

One, maybe two, time I kinda drop off to sleep. I keep thinkin' when that happen, we 'seem to back up 'cause, like Lack say, we goin' upstream. This gonna be a long trip.

"Lack, git up. Time I git some sleep."

"I ain't finish yet."

"You git up."

I told Lack 'bout the boat goin' backward and I figure we was gonna have to change more quicker. He say OK and it work jus' fine. Still it was slow goin' and I figure my arms was 'bout to drop off. I look at the watch and I seen we gotta whole day to go.

We git used to changin' every hour so we kep' on doin' it. That food pretty Lucille give us was real good and it was holdin' up real nice. I begin wonderin' how long food stay fit to eat. I 'member some o' them fattenin' pigs Pa usta keep jus' drop over dead. Pa say they ketch food poison. Pa begin smellin' our pig feed and we throw 'way what Pa say gone bad. I told Lack wonder did Charlie eat some bad food and ketch food poison. Lack said maybe we oughta smell all our food bags once in awhile.

I was sleep and Lack yell at me, "Homer. Wake up. I think we home."

"Home? You mean Dodgetown?"

"No, Homer. This our new home. We fixin' to pull in. See. There the big **B** mark."

I reach up and pat Lack on his shoulder. "OK. Go in the channel and slow down. Watch out for people ain't sposed to be there."

Lack paddle up the channel and run in the little door. We come over to the dock and here come Ed. "You're back. Ahead of schedule. Didn't expect you until six or seven. You boys go to your room and get plenty of sleep. Be back in the morning. You gotta a real run head of you."

Chapter 18

"Oconee Trail"

@Anonymous

Next mornin' my arm was sore as a half-day mule doin' a two-day trot. "Hey, Ed. Ain't itta good day outside? Air so nice and cool. Make me want to git my cane pole and go ketch a mess o' fish."

"One of these days, Homer, you and Lack and I will get in one of my boats and we'll take a run over to High Road River. Some of the tributaries of that river have still-water coves where the finest bream in the world school. Old Charlie told me he came back once with over a hundred beautiful plump fish after a single afternoon of fishing. He said it seemed as if the fish just jumped in the boat."

"I hope we do that, Ed."

"Come in my office, boys. Got something now that's a lot more interesting. Your next mission. In fact, your most important mission."

Ed unlock the door and me and Lack went in. They was this great big map settin' on top the big table in the middle o' his office. "That a real map, Ed?"

"Yep, but don't get excited about something you don't understand yet. First I'll tell you the secret part that you may never speak to anyone about. OK? Never?"

"Yep, Ed. You payin' our way. We work jus' for you."

"OK. Here is the reason we're in business. We think the Yankees are about to push south, maybe toward Atlanta. They might attack some of the storage facilities where Confederate material and supplies are stockpiled. If they succeed, that could end the Confederacy."

"I git my gun and go up there."

"No, Lack. No. Our job is to stop them another way. You boys want some more runs to Dahlonega? And go places you've never been?"

"Dahlonega? We was there when we was boat-trainin'? The one had the **A** marker?"

"Yes. Station **A**. Remember you brought back some empty boxes back. Right?"

"Yep, I 'member."

"Well, we'll be doing that over and again. But from now on we'll also be doing other things. We'll be hauling all sorts of material from Dahlonega and taking it where the Yankees won't find it. I'm talking about important material, including war supplies, of the CSA. And, as usual, you may never, ever open or look inside any box you are transporting. Remember that."

"Blest Pete, Ed. Reckon thatta final git us that parade when we git home? And do a shootin' show?"

"Parade? You do your job and don't ever divulge this secret and I'll be sure you get what you deserve."

Me and Lack both blab 'bout we gonna help anyway we kin. We said he oughta quit all his hem hawin' round and less git goin'. Lack begin hittin' me on my shoulder. "Homer, look like we final gonna git that parade and I betcha I be champ o' that shootin' show."

"We'll see if we can arrange a real celebration. But we have to do our job first."

"Where we goin', Ed?"

"You know our main headquarters is right here in Gainesville. Marker **B**. Right? We call it home base. You boys will be on the move a lot. Not much time off."

"Ed, one o' these days I wanna play some more o' that baseball game."

"We'll do that. But for now, we have a lot of work to do. And because of all that extra work, I am givin' each of you a pay raise. You've been receiving ten dollars a week up until now. That goes up to twenty dollars a week right now."

"Twenty? Thank you, Ed. We gonna feel like we rich."

"It'll be worth it with all the time you're putting in. Now, come out here in the boat bay. You boys now have your own boat. Right here."

"That gonna 'long to me and Homer?"

"Yep. B-21 is your boat. Old B-11 was just a trainer. Now, boys, look. This is the bow. The very forward part of the boat. See this little flag standing up straight? What's the number on it?"

"It say B, a two, and a one. Our own number, Ed?"

"Nobody elses. Based in Gainesville. Look how this flag comes off quickly. Now you see it. Pull it out and now you don't."

"How come that?"

"If you're on the river and you see something suspicious, such as maybe a Yankee patrol or some renegades, just take out the flag and stow it right in this little compartment. Then pick up this fishing gear and pretend to be fishing. That's why we run real quietly and mostly at night near army bases and towns."

"What all kinda other places we gonna run to, Ed?"

"You will learn that only when you're assigned. Even though you have been judged to know your job, with authority to hear classified information, we only divulge information on what we call a *need to know basis*. If Jeff Davis was to come by today, we couldn't tell him."

"You mean we might know somethin' Jeff Davis don't?"

"Absolutely!"

"Sound good to me, Ed. But somehow I gotta hard time knowin' 'bout some o' them things you talkin' 'bout."

"Homer. Here's the main thing. Don't tell a soul anything you hear or see. Whatever it is."

"We do that, Ed."

"And if somebody starts to ask questions about what you are doing, where you are going, what you are hauling, or anything like that, tell me immediately. OK?"

"We do it, Ed."

"Good. It's after three o'clock now. You boys take off this afternoon and get some rest and good food. We'll get B-21 ready to go. In the morning, eat breakfast at seven and pick up two food bags apiece from Mrs. Wilkes and be back here at eight. We'll go over your mission facts. You will leave not later than nine o'clock. Now, go get some rest."

We walk 'cross the street and begin talkin' to one 'nuther. "Lack, how come Ed so good to us. Up and give us a raise and a whole boat."

"I reckon he like us. I can't wait to git home to Dodgetown and have us that parade and a shootin' show. I know I kin win the shootin' show, Homer, even if Billy git in it."

"I hope so. Maybe after we done eatin', we oughta set down real quiet like and think 'bout do we think is all this real or not. Lotta bent people in the world today, Lack."

"I don't think Ed one o' them."

We eat some o' Mrs. Wilkes' good food and went over to our room. When we laid down on them beds to rest, both of us musta jus' plain pass out. I come wide 'wake when it was 'bout one o'clock in the mornin'. I look over at Lack and seen his mouth was wide open, jus' like it always stay when he sleep. I wish I could learn that boy some good manners. Sometime he go to sleep in that boat house, settin' straight up, and his mouth come wide open. Ed always make fun o' him. I hate it, 'cause it give me shame o' my own blood brother. I hate to think 'bout one day when we git that parade and shootin' show in Dodgetown and all the folks 'round home gonna look at Lack and make fun of him. I figure I wadn't gonna wake him up and talk 'bout our worry 'bout is Ed a good man. Maybe I wait till we out on the river.

Me and Lack git up 'round six o'clock and go down to Mrs. Wilkes' food table. She musta knowed we was goin' on a long trip 'cause she done scramble up a bunch o' eggs, cook a mess o' bacon and sausage, and boil a whole pot o' yellow grits. When you drop a some o' them grits on your plate, they stand straight up like a mountain. And stay straight up. On the table I seen a bunch o' brown biscuits. They look jus' like Ma's. Waitin' to sop up all the sorghum in that jug.

"Lack, we can't keep eatin' no more. Ed wanna see us 'bout eight. We oughta git there 'fore eight. That way, he know we like him. Less git our food bags and go."

It was little 'fore eight when we git to the boat place and Ed was showin' them men 'bout puttin' them boxes in B-21. They git six boxes spread out in the boat and that boat begin to ride real low in the water.

"Ed, what we gonna do if this boat start sinkin'? Or run up on a gator?"

"Only way that'll happen is if you hit something like a sharp tree stump just under the water. And then it's not likely you'll be going fast enough for a stump to break through the boat bottom anyway. A gator will move away from the boat if you get too close. Just don't go swimming."

"I see a gator, Ed, and I ain't even gonna stick my finger near no water."

"You boys ready to roll?"

"Yep. Where we goin'? It ain't far from nine right now."

Ed run his hand over that map on the table. "You'll be takin' this load of boxes to Dublin. Station **E**. Boys, Dublin is exactly 160 miles from here. That's a long way. How long will it take, Lack? Remember the Oconee is flowing at one mile per hour and you boys can paddle at three."

"Ain't no problem, Ed. We gonna take 40 hour to git there."

"Forty hour," I yelled out at Lack. "Close to two whole day o' straight runnin'. How long gonna be to git back?"

"Tell him, Lack."

"Thatta be 80 hour."

"Blest Pete, Ed. We gonna be on the water a long time?"

"But, on the way down, I suggest you break it up in two legs. The first will be the same one you did a few days ago to Milledgeville. Remember Station **D**?"

"Yep. I 'member. That where Lucille give us all that good food."

"You can't travel all the way in one stop. So, stop at Station **D**, Milledgeville, and sleep for a few hours and get a good meal. Remember, you've been there before. Carl is manager and Lucille runs the lodging. Then you'll get up early and head for Dublin."

"Gonna be a long trip, Ed."

"Right. Lack could tell us that the run from Station **D** in Milledgeville to Station **E** in Dublin is 47 miles. Lack could tell us that, going downstream, the run time is a little over 10 hours."

"Ed, only watch we got is Charlie's. Reckon we need 'nuther one?"

"No. Charlie's is a good watch. Don't tell me you boys are getting nervous about these long runs."

"Kinda scary thinkin' 'bout if that watch come off my arm and drop in the river. How we gonna know nuthin'?"

"You boys can do it. Look at this little map you'll be carrying. You'll come into Dublin where the Oconee does kind of a turn to right turn then a circle turn to port. See this? Run until you go under the bridge. That is right in the center of town. Right here.

"Now, keep going for about 200 yards, then move over to port, or left side of the river. Right about here. You know how far 200 yards is?"

"Yep. Ed. Both us does."

"At 200 yards past the bridge, on the port side, the east side, you'll see a tall telegraph pole sticking almost out of the river. Look ten feet high for the white square marker with a black '**E**' on it."

"Thass where we turn, Ed?"

"That's where you turn in, to the left, to port. Won't be any trouble seeing the channel running between two young magnolia trees. Paddle about twenty feet up the channel and pass under a canvas flap, just like before. Look for George. He runs the place. He'll direct you to Rachael's Place. You'll eat and stay there overnight and return the next day. Right now we think we'll have empty boxes, but that might change. George will know. Any questions?"

"Ed, what all this 'bout? What we gonna carry?"

"You boys remember. We load the boats. And you deliver it. OK?"

"I reckon I oughta quit gittin' curious, Ed. When we leave?"

"Be ready at nine o'clock on the dot. Your boat is ready. You have the map and your food bags from Mrs. Wilkes. You boys have a long haul, so better get started."

We begin the run and both o' us stay kinda edgy. We ain't run boats this far 'way from home 'fore in all our whole life. We ain't been to most o' them places we goin' to. Lack say it give him some o' them willies like Ma used to talk 'bout when she pick beans at night in the field.

We was lucky 'cause we done been to Milledgeville one time. Carl. He run the boat place and that pretty Lucille cook the food and give us a bed. I be glad to see that lady 'gain. Pretty lady like that kin plain make a boy get happy and joyful when he scared and nervous.

"When we gonna git to Milledgeville, Lack?"

"Runnin' time ten hours. Mean we oughta pull in seven o'clock tonight. I kin jus' 'magine what Lucille got waitin' for us."

"I be glad too."

We run south and makin' good time. I kep' on lookin' at them boxes and wond'rin' what was in 'em. A little rainstorm come up and git me and Lack kinda chilly.

'Bout four 'clock in the afternoon, cold as it was, we git to makin' good time. Lack was runnin' the boat and I was half-sleep, waitin' for him to wake up and take over. "Look, Homer. A boat. Ain't it funny. Only one we seen yet."

"Yeh. Somebody fishin' and maybe he 'cidin' to change spots or go home. If I be him, I be headin' home. See they two people in that boat. They fishin' 'cause them fishin' poles is stickin' up." We begin wishin' we wudda brung some poles 'long with us.

It git nearbout 6:30 and dark, and Lack was sleep so I git him up. "Gotta find marker **D**, Lack. 'Bout time to git some rest and eat some 'o Lucille's good food."

"I see it, Homer. Them big granite rocks stickin' up."

"Thass it, Lack. Guide us over to starboard."

We run under that flap, up the channel, in the boat house, and here come Carl. "Y'all git here OK."

"Ain't got no reason we wuddn't, Carl. Lucille got some good stuff left?"

"Lucille got good food all the time."

Carl taken our boat and dock it in a safe place where ain't nobody kin see it. We walk over and eat a real good supper. Lucille set down at the table with us some and while we was talkin' I seen again she was pretty as Pauline. She tell us our bed all fixed and she sposed to git us up at six in the mornin'.

I laid on my bed for a hour thinkin' 'bout which was prettiest. Lucille or Pauline. Then I said neither one. Jeannie, back at school, was most pretty. I musta dreamed it all through the night, 'cause ever' time I come half wake I seen her. There she was, pretty as ever. Them was good dreams.

Chapter 19

"Oconee Trail"

@Anonymous

I begin hearin' rapping on the door. It was Lucille, yellin' it was six clock and she got us some good breakfast. Me and Lack git up and she was right. We eat some o' that juicy breakfast. Lack, jus' like hisself, eat too much, and I knowed I be the one to paddle that boat by myself till he get straight.

We git over to the boat shed and Carl already git B-21 to the dock, ready to go. "Carl, I been kinda nervous. We gotta go where we ain't never been yet."

"Ain't no problem. You boys done run more'n all our crews. You doin' fine."

"Y'all got more people on the river than me and Lack?"

"Sure. Ain't no way you and Lack kin do everything we got to do if we ain't got but one crew?"

"What we seen yesterday afternoon musta been 'nuther crew runnin', Lack."

"OK. Homer. You boys ready?"

"We ready to git goin', Carl. Scared or not."

Right on the dot, seven 'clock, and sun barely showin' when we run down that channel. We turn starboard and hit the Oconee and head for Dublin, or like Ed say, station **E**. Must be a big bunch o' people Ed got runnin' the river, haulin' them boxes. Blest Pete, ain't nobody kin see what's in 'em. Lack, he don't give a hoot. I do.

I can't figure out how come me and Lack git lucky 'nuff to be doin' what we doin' and makin' money and gittin' to run boats. We ain't done no fishin' yet, but Ed, he say one day we gonna go fish in that High Road River, where all them coves is, and rake in a mighty mess o' *brim*.

I figure we was half way to Dublin when I look at Charlie's watch. Yep, we was half way 'cause it was noon time. Lack say itta be ten hours goin' from Milledgeville to Dublin so we oughta git to Dublin 'bout 5:00 if we don't sink. Storm clouds come rollin' in and the wind raise up strong and brung on rain. Cold like it was, we sposed not to let nuthin' stop us, so we kep' on goin'.

Reckon the bad weather git the bes' of Lack and he raise up outta his sleep. "We got any coats, Homer?"

"No. We got 'em all on. Noon now, Lack. Dinner time. We half way. Git some food outta them bags. You gotta take a turn in a minute. Wish we wudda git Ed to give us some raincoats like the Army got. If I'da knowed we was gonna be doin' this stuff, I wudda git some from Gunny 'fore we left."

"Homer, look back o' us! Look like 'nuther fishin' boat. Got fishin' poles stickin' up. If them people ain't a fool, I never seen none. Least they cudda wait till the rain stop. They gonna ketch the croup 'stead o' fish."

"Lack. That the same boat as 'fore?"

"Look like it. Only thing, this fur 'way, boats look like one 'nuther. Like Gunny say 'bout pretty ladies, 'they all look like'."

"OK, Lack. Git me up at two. Keep steady movin'. We gotta show Ed we kin do anythin' he want us to. Think 'bout how proud Pa and Lotta gonna be when we ridin' in that p'rade and shootin' in that shootin' show."

"I know I kin win the shootin' show, Homer."

"'Member, Lack. Two o'clock."

I laid down and the rain kep' a comin'. I look down and sleet was stickin' to my blanket. Least it wadn't comin' all the way through. I kep' thinkin' 'bout what was we doin'. Blest Pete. Ed ain't told us nuthin'. We oughta know what we doin'. Anyway, Ed, he a real good man and payin' me and Lack a heap so I don't wanna stir up no problem and git fired and then we won't git nuthin'.

"Homer. Git up. Two 'clock, 'coordin' to the watch." Old Lack was dead on the money. I ain't got no idea how he knowed it 'cause he ain't got no watch.

"It quit rainin', Lack."

"Yeh, and sky done cleared up. Only it ain't git'n no warmer."

"Where that fishin' boat go? Rain quit. Clear now. We oughta see 'im."

"'Bout a hour after you went to 'sleep, I cudn't see him no more. Reckon he git tired o' puttin' up with the rain and cold."

"OK, Lack. Go to sleep. Two hour. If we git a problem, I be yellin'." Musta been half a minute when Lack laid down and he git to snorin' and his mouth come wide open. But he wadn't eatin' no flies this time 'cause flies freeze in this weather 'fore you kin eat 'em.

The river was gittin' bigger, more south we run. Pretty too. Them big poplar trees was tall to the sky and they was mixin' in real friendly-like with them pines. I seen lots o' loblollies and longleafs. I hope them people livin' 'round here knowed 'bout all this pretty stuff too.

There! There that same boat again, or could be 'nuther one. Cudn't tell 'cause it was too far off. Still fishin'. I kin see them fishin' poles. How come them men puttin' up with all that rain? Wish I could bring a pole on a run soon.

Time kinda slip away and I seen this kinda big lookin' town side of the river we comin' to the middle of. Charlie's watch say it ain't far from 5:00. That when Lack say we sposed to git to Dublin.

"Lack. Git up."

"Where we at?"

"Dublin, I think. Ed call it station **E**. I reckon thass where we at."

"Yeh, Homer. Look. Comin' up on a big bridge and the river doin' a kind of a turn to starboard and then a humpback circle to port. Jus' like Ed said."

"You gittin' good, Lack. We gotta keep goin' till we git 200 yards past the bridge. Keep paddlin'."

"Homer, look there. That pole. It gotta **E** on it. Look. Told you."

"I see it, Lack. Quit yellin' it out. Ed say don't let on nuthin' to nobody. Little bit more we sposed to turn port. 'Tween them magnolias. Now!"

"Lemme take it in, Homer. I like goin' under them canvas flaps. Keep your gun ready."

"Doin' good. Paddle some more."

"Made it, Homer. We in the boat shed. We done it.'"

"Reckon that mus' be George comin' over. Hey, you George?"

"Hey, Boys. Yep, my name George. Guess you Homer and Lack."

"Yeh. Here the papers Ed sent."

"You boys done a good job. We gonna telegraph Ed right now. You boys seen anything strange out on the river?"

"Naw. Jus' a little boat. Size of a fishin' boat."

"Where?"

"Seen one yesterday 'fore we git to Milledgeville. 'Nuther one nearby us most o' the run today. Mighta been the same one."

"He git close?"

"Naw. Look like he was jus' fishin'. Funny with all that sleet goin' on."

"If he ever git to closin' in, use them guns."

"Who we gonna shoot?"

"Ed say somebody told him some French army people might come up close and try to steal whatever in our boats. He don't know for sure 'bout that, but thass what he told me."

"Blest Pete. I reckon this turnin' a mite risky, George."

"You OK right now. Go git some o' Rachaels's food and sleep some and you be in good shape."

"Where she at?"

"Yonder. Cross the street. See that big white sign with big black writin'? Thass it. She know you comin'. Now, git outta here and be back 'bout seven in the mornin'."

"Let's go, Lack. You reckon this gonna be like the army and us gittin' shot at like we done up at Ball's Bluff?"

"Somebody shoot me, he gonna git it two times back. Jus' like we done at Ball's Bluff."

We open the door and smell in a real fine scent. Bacon and sausage and eggs. Settin' on a table we seen some biscuits so big I cudda wore like shoes. And a whole pan of yellow grits was yellin' at me and Lack to fill up with. That sorghum syrup was achin' to git sopped up.

"Hello, boys. You must be Homer and Lack from over at George's."

"Yes, ma'am. He say you gonna feed us and sleep us."

"You ready to eat right now?"

"Yes ma'am."

Rachael give each us a metal food pan like the army got and we soon gittin' what we like first. Lack musta had a real hankerin' for bacon today 'cause I look at his pan and thass all I seen. We final git full, but 'fore we git up, Lack taken one o' them big biscuits, poke his finger in one end, and pour it full o' sorghum.

Rachael crook her finger at us so we come along. She kinda look like Pauline from back at Sparta. While we was walkin', Lack kep' eatin' on his biscuit till the syrup leak out and run down all over his hand. The room we git was upstairs and mighty nice. Both us git our own bed and Rachael show us a bathin' room down the hall. 'Fore I knowed it, Lack done pull off his clothes, run down to where the tub is, wash his self, and come back to our room. Nekkid as a jaybird. I hope nobody seen him. Not more'n a minute after that, he drop right in bed and his eyes slam shut. I kep' thinkin' I was so tired I wish I could sleep fast as that boy kin.

I reckon I sleep pretty good 'cause I ain't hear nuthin' till I wake up when a loud knock come on the door and I yell, "Who knockin'?" Blest Pete, it was Rachael tellin' us to git up 'cause she got food on the table. I tell you, Ed know how to pick them food and sleepin' people. Ain't no way I could 'cide which o' them food places Ed got was better'n next one.

Me and Lack git up, dress up, and went to the food place to eat some breakfast. This time when we finish eatin', Lack poke holes in two biscuits and filled 'em up with sorghum. We come back to the boat shed and Carl said he got some news on the telegraph from Ed. He said we ain't likely gonna like it, but we ain't goin' back to Gainesville right now. Ed give us orders to load up B-21 with a big bunch of them boxes and take 'em down to Darien and unload 'em.

"How far that, Carl?"

"This what you ain't gonna like. Close to 150 miles."

"Homer," said Lack. "That many miles mean it take close to forty hour to git there." I still can't believe how fas' that boy come up with them answers.

"Little over 40 hours, Lack? Spose how long to git back?"

"'Bout 80 hours."

"That don't seem right, Lack."

"He right as rain," said Carl. "Water goin' one mile a hour and you boys paddlin' three mile a hour mean your boat go four mile a hour. Jus' don't think 'bout gittin' back. This your job. You lucky you ain't got to go home and git fussed at from no woman."

"We gonna git us a map?"

Carl pull out some maps and lay 'em out on the table. "Yep. These here some good maps. Yall gotta learn 'bout 'em 'fore you go. You be runnin' the Oconee down to Glenwood right here at Station **F**," he said, pointin' his finger, "and then it gonna turn in to a big river they call the Altamaha. You foller it all the way to Station **G** and after that Station **H** in Darien. Talk 'bout fish! *Brim* big as whales all long the way."

"We ain't run nothin' this hard yet. That 'bout to the ocean, ain't it?"

"You right, boy, but you kin do it. These maps is good. Can't find no faults on 'em. While our boys finish loadin' up, less look hard at 'em and see what you gotta do to git there and git back."

Carl pat us on the back and give us good luck. Lack git up front in the boat and I push off to the channel. Wudn't but a minute we come to the Oconee, turn to port, and was sayin' bye to Dublin. I ain't had no tellin' how long it gonna be till we come back up this way.

"Jus' you and me, Lack. How long it is till we get to the first stop."

"Thirty mile to Station **F**, Homer. 'Bout seven hours. Put us there 'round 2:00. We gonna need to dig in our food bag 'fore we git there."

"Carl say Jim is manager and Ruth make the food. Reckon she pretty?"

"Probly be like Pauline is. I think I git some rest, Homer. OK?"

Lack was jus' like he always done; sleep in one minute. Least it wadn't rainy. Kinda cold, but wudn't no rain. Seem like all the deer come out today, drinkin' up the Oconee. I kep' on lookin' for some o' them other boats. Funny. Ain't none showed hisself all day and it was 'bout noon now.

"Lack. Git up."

"We got trouble?"

"No. Time we git in them food bags. I been lookin' at it but I 'cided you oughta open it." We eat some stuff outta Rachael's food bag and it was good as all the rest of 'em. Yep. Ed got some good food ladies.

We pull in to Station **F** right on time. We git there and wadn't nobody 'round, but directly this big tall man come over. He never look like his name was Jim, but Pa usta say you can't tell nobody's name from how they look. "You Jim?"

"I ain't nobody else. 'Course I'm Jim. You in Glenwood now. Reckon you Lack and Homer."

"Yep. Me and Lack git a load of stuff to go to Darien. Them maps tell us we got a long way to go."

"Eighty mile to Jesup, then nearbout fifty more to Darien."

"Ed say we probly wanna jus' stop off for a minute here 'fore we go on to Jesup. We figure we git to Jesup 'bout midnight and rest."

"You seen any strange boats on the way down?"

"Not since yestiddy. Any 'round here anywhere?"

"Yeh, some folks say they seen some. Mighta been fishin'. Reckon you bes' wait till dark?"

"Ed, he say them boxes gotta git down in a hurry."

"You boys know what them boxes got in 'em?"

"Ed told us we ain't got no reason knowin', so we sposed to not ask no more or we gonna git fired."

"Don't it rile you up?"

"No. This only way I kin make a livin'."

"I git all rile up when somethin' strange goin' on and I wanna know."

"Be careful, Jim. Ruth, she git some food bags ready?"

"Ruth gone."

"Comin' back?"

"I don't know."

"Then we gotta go on. Ed, he give us a order to git this load to Darien fast."

Me and Lack start gittin' old B-21 ready and Jim kep' sayin' not to go. He kinda grab Lack like he was tryin' to make 'im stay, but I stick up my gun and Jim back off. None o' this was nowhere close to what Ed told us none of his men sposed to do.

I motion to Lack to git in the boat and paddle. I reckon Jim wadn't too stuck on us stayin' so he leave us alone and Bless Pete, wadn't long 'fore we was in a great big river where Carl say we was gonna see the

Oconee and the Ocmulgee run together and make a big'n name of the Altamaha. We got to 'member this when we come back.

"Lack. What we got in the food bag?"

"I eat it all this mornin', Homer."

"Means we ain't got nothin' left. We gotta watch for some deer or somethin'."

I knowed we was in a mess. Bother me 'bout how Jim act. He nervous as a beddin' rabbit. I kep' thinkin' 'bout it but we ain't never been down this way 'fore, so I was nervous 'bout a lotta things. We gonna run to midnight without no food don't we find somethin' drinkin' on the river bank. We both paddle fast so we git there sooner. I told Lack lets run on the side of the river where lotsa bushes is.

Wadn't long 'fore it was close to 6:00 and the sun settlin' down fast. I seen somethin' move and look up and Blest Pete, I seen a 'coon on the edge o' the water. He was splashin' his front feet in the water like some people say he do when he washin' his food. "Lack. Git your gun, now."

"What, Homer?"

"See that 'coon. "Bout thirty yards off to the right? On the bank, washin'."

"Yep."

"Shoot 'im. Now."

'Fore you know it, Lack done shot and that 'coon was layin' upside down with his feet stickin' straight up. We paddle over and he wadn't even flinchin' none. He was dead like a doornail. Lack git out his knife and begin skinnin' and guttin' him and both us could taste a good meal comin' up. We found a landin' place and git us a fire goin' with a 'coon roastin' on it. 'Minded us 'bout them ducks we cook 'fore we git to Milledgeville last August.

A hour later we done eat every last drop o' that coon and was headin' south again. "Lucky we saw him when we did, Lack. Done git dark now and we wudn't have no more chance. OK, git paddlin'."

We pull in to Jesup 'bout 1:00 in the mornin', 'bout a hour late, and come in the channel to Station **G.** We figure we was gonna hafta wait till mornin', but here come a man runnin' over to us. "You Homer?"

"Yep. Homer and Lack. You Ralph?"

"Yep. You late."

"We run into a fussy man at Station **F.** Jim he say his name was but he begin talkin' 'bout things Ed say not to never talk 'bout."

"Old Jim got his own mind and it don't always run straight with Ed. I kinda worry 'bout what all goin' on with him. He don't mind talkin' out what lay on his mind. He gonna be sorry 'bout that one day."

"He bad?"

"No. A good man. I trust him pretty good. Jus' his mind don't always run with Ed and he don't mind talkin' 'bout it."

"So we jus' raise up our gun and git in the boat and paddle off. He stand there a minute. Somethin' wrong doin' that?"

"I reckon. He really OK. Treat 'im nice when you go back. Come on in and see Alice. She git you some eats and some beds. All that stuff you done, you lucky be jus' a hour late. Real good. I git off a telegraph in the mornin'. Yep, Jim a good man."

Alice cook like all the rest and she pretty too. Food wadn't new-fresh but me and Lack put away lots o' rations. Alice set down and talk with us 'bout how come we work so hard. I told her we ain't got no other way to make no livin'. She talk 'bout where we live and how come we don't quit and go back. Lack pipe right up and say we gonna go back and have a p'rade and a shootin' show. When we leave we was real good friends.

We come back to the boat shed and told Ralph it was close to 2:00 now and we promise Ed we gonna get down to Darien real fast, so we movin' on. He say OK, but don't think bad o' Jim.

We paddle fast and the sun come up 'bout 6:30 in the mornin'. We figure we was still four hours short o' Darien. We eat a good helpin' outta that food bag Alice give us. We kep' paddlin' faster, and git to Darien little after 10:00. Grady, he run the place, come over and look real close at them boxes. He told us to go over in a minute and git Helen to show us where the food stay.

"Ed say I sposed to send you boys on back to Gainesville. Helen gonna wake you up 'bout six in the mornin'. You git some eatin' done and be ready to get on the river at 7:00. Got any questions?"

"No, Grady. We do jus' what we told to. We ready for bed now."

We walk over kinda slow. "Lack, what we doin' here? We in a big mess?"

"Naw. I like this job, Homer."

"We'll see."

Chapter 20

"Oconee Trail"

@Anonymous

I raise up and somebody was pokin' and shakin' me and yellin' real loud. First thing, I figure some Yankee done git after me or it could be one o' them bears they got down in these parts. Then I seen Lack was doin' it. "Lack! Somethin' wrong with you?"

"Somebody knockin' on the door, Homer."

"Well, go see who."

It was that nice lady, Helen. She said time to git up 'cause Grady want us to git to the boat shed so we kin be on the way by 7:00. We eat breakfast too fast to have fun at it, but it taste jus' as good as all them other places. Helen give us three food bags. "You boys gotta long run 'head o' you."

While we was walkin' to the shed, I told Lack don't mention nothin' 'bout what we been sayin' 'bout Jim and don't make no mention 'bout Charlie neither. "More I hear 'bout what mighta happen to Charlie, more I hope nuthin' like that ain't gonna happen to you and me."

"What, Homer?"

"I don't know. Jim say he think somethin' lowly happen to Charlie. Jim better be watchin' what he say, don't somethin' gonna happen to him, too."

"How come somebody would up and do somethin' to good ol' Charlie?"

"Nobody don't actual know what happen to Charlie. But nobody better be goin' 'round tellin' secret boat stuff. Lack, right now lemmee tell you. Don't make no mention a'tall 'bout Charlie and nuthin' 'bout boats or nuthin' else. To nobody. OK?"

Grady come in and we shut up. "Mornin' boys. You ready to go?"

"We ready, Grady. Gonna be slow movin' uphill. A whole day jus' gittin' back to where Ralph at. We gonna haul any stuff?"

"Naw. All stuff comin' south now. We ain't sendin' nuthin' north right now. B-21 ready to roll. You boys be extry careful."

We pull out and done a port turn and head north up the Altamaha. Lack laid down to git the first nap. Wadn't no time he was snorin'. I kep' lookin' at them trees on the bank. Lack was right. The stream goin' jus' one mile 'gainst us make a whole heap o' difference. 'Bout a hour later, Lack raise up and look all 'round.

"How we doin', Homer. We at Jesup yet?"

"No. Ain't but 8:00 right now. Only been gone a hour. We ain't gonna be to Jesup till 'bout this time tomorrow."

"I better git my stick and both us paddle."

"No, Lack. You paddle when I lay down."

Old Lack ain't change one bit the whole trip. He still sleep time he lay down. I look over and see them deer still comin' down by the river drinkin' and I keep thinkin' how nice itta be to git a big hunk o' deer meat.

My mind drift off to poor old Charlie and all Jim and Grady been hintin' at. Fact is, I ain't really got no strong idea 'bout the meanin'. I told Lack it kinda be like Ma usta tell us kids. Keep your mouth shut and your eyes open, 'cause that way you learn a lot and not git in no trouble. Ain't it funny how smart Ma was.

'Bout 12:00, Lack set straight up like he ain't got no idea 'bout where he is. First thing he say was he ain't got no idea 'bout where we is and he hungry. I told him to git some food. He eat some mixed ham and potatoes and some beans and cornbread. He drink a dipper o' river water and say he wish he could lay down longer. I told 'im it ain't his time, so we trade off all the way to Jesup.

'Bout 8:00 a.m., we pull in to Jesup. Ralph meet us and sent us over to Alice to git some food and sleep some. My ears stay open but so far I ain't hear nuthin' more 'bout no secret stuff.

Alice git us up at 4:00 p.m. and we git ready for a long run up to Station **F,** Glenwood, where Jim and Ruth at. That a two-day trip, so Alice give us five food bags. She say the weather cold so itta keep. That trip the longest one in all the ones we run in.

When we was comin' close to Glenwood, I told Lack the days gittin' near Christmas 'cause this the first day of December and how we usta have a good Christmas time back home. We git to the channel where we turn in and my tired arms cudn't hardly make it no longer. Bes' thing I was lookin' for was how was Jim and Ruth. We pull up the channel and go in the boat shed. The door open and a kinda young man come over. "You Homer and Lack?"

"Yep. Where Jim?"

"He ain't here no more. My name Hank."

"Jim ain't? Alice?"

"She ain't neither. Martha taken her place."

"Where they go?"

"Only thing I know, she cook up a pot o' 'coon a week ago. I wadn't here but people been talkin' 'bout it wadn't no boats come in that day, and the 'coon musta go rotten and they musta eat some and caught food poison. Somebody come git 'em and bury 'em up on the hill."

"Martha git some new food made up?"

"Yep. Cook it today. She gonna fix you a sleepin' place and git you some food bags. Ed send a message 'bout y'all boat drivers hurry and git up to Gainesville fast 'cause some more runs gotta git made."

"Martha gonna wake us up like them other ladies done?"

"Yep. Don't, she git fired."

Me and Lack eat and git to our room and was takin' off our shirt and pants to git to sleep. Lack say real low, "Homer, ain't bad food what happen to Charlie?"

"Yep. Don't say nothing 'bout it a'tall to nobody. Not no word till jus' me and you is on the river. Now lay down and git to sleep. We hadda long day, two day worth. More to come."

We left out in the mornin' and Lack paddle first. Hank 'minded us we gotta branch off the Altamaha to starboard to git back on the Oconee. A whole day and a half later, when we git to Dublin, we come right through the middle o' town and pull in to Station **E**. George come over and told us to git on over to Rachael's and git filled up with barbecue. Wadn't nobody else 'round and I 'cided to say somethin' to George 'bout what happen to Jim.

George say real quiet, "Homer. You oughta not be talkin' 'bout nothin' like that."

"You got some doubtin', George?"

"I ain't gonna say no more. Bes' thing is, you and Lack shut up and get some rest and be on the way in the mornin' to Milledgeville, Station **D**. You git what I say?"

"I git it, George. Kin we leave early in the mornin'?"

"We be ready. I tell Rachael what time."

Next mornin', Rachael was ready and give us four food bags. Me and Lack told George bye and I begin paddlin' north. We got two days to git to Station **D**, Milledgeville. Lack say we oughta git there 'bout 5:00 in the mornin'. I tell 'im that was where Gunny give us all that army trainin' and it wudda been good if he hadda been there too. We talk 'bout the captain and how we never seen him much at trainin' time. And when we was in Sparta that day, he took to hangin' 'round Pauline a heap.

"Lack. Way them two was actin', I say them was good friends or wanna be. 'Cept they cudn't be 'cause he a Rebel and Pauline git flat caught 'cause she a Yankee spy. Reckon they was jus' friends?"

"Maybe so or somethin' worser, Homer."

Worser? When Lack say that, I jus' set there thinkin' for a minute. Dumb as Lack kin be, maybe he got a few brains left in hisself. "Reckon you right, Lack?"

"'Member Ma usta say anythin' possible. Why it ain't?"

Me and Lack make good time switchin' and headin' north and my mind kep' thinkin' a heap. One day go by, then a few hours more to Milledgeville. We keep on talkin' and thinkin' 'bout what goin' on. Charlie, Jim, the captain, and Pauline. "How we gonna figure it out, Homer?"

"I don't know, Lack. Who gonna listen?"

"'Member how Ma usta say *anythin' possible*?"

"I wish old Gunny was still at that army camp in Milledgeville. Hey! Maybe he done come back from Virginia like he sposed to. Lack, reckon we oughta go see is he back?"

"Do and we might git in high trouble. Anyway, how we gonna do that, Homer?"

"How far to Milledgeville?"

"Git there 5:00 in the mornin'."

"Lack, reckon we oughta hide the boat in the bushes outside o' Milledgeville and go find that trainin' camp? It ain't far from the river. Two mile, I think. We might find Gunny. Hallelujah, Lack! I like that!"

Me and Lack kep' makin' good time and we ain't stop talkin' 'bout them things keep goin' on and if we right, it ain't good for the South. We ain't got no idea what Ed got in them boxes we haulin'. "Lack, we got one big question and we gotta git a answer to it. What them boxes got in 'em?"

"Maybe we oughta open one of 'em."

"Shudda done it 'fore now. We only got empty boxes. Only way we kin do it now is go back to Gainesville and git 'nuther load and do it then. That gonna take over a week."

"Less do it thattaway, Homer."

"With all them people gittin' dead, Lack, we ain't got 'nuff time."

"I don't want nobody killin' me and you 'fore we git our p'rade and shootin' show."

"Less keep talkin' 'bout it. Pa always say somebody need to think things out 'fore he actual do it. We got half the night left till 5:00 in the mornin'."

More we talk, more all kinda things come to mind. "Lack, we can't snub no idea pop in our head. Might jus' be the bes' one." Stuff kep' comin' in and out, but nuthin' come up no better'n stoppin' in Milledgeville and seein' is Gunny back.

Charlie's watch say 5:10 when we seen the bridge way 'fore we git to Milledgeville. Me and Lack both 'member them tall rocks where Station **D** is, north o' the bridge, on the west side. "Lack, we gotta pull over to to the east side o' the river and tie it up 'fore we git near them rocks."

It was gittin' dawn and we could see tolerable. We seen this good place and git the boat hid in the bushes near the bridge, 'cross from Station **D**. Ain't no Yankee or nobody kin see it, special not Ed. We eat most o' what was left in the food bags and begin lookin' for how to git to the army base. Bes' thing was I 'member the water tower I seen when me and Billy and them other boys was crossin' over the bridge, goin' to the camp.

We climb up the river cliff and seen the road goin' east. So we gotta walk for two miles to git to the camp. Only this time we stay inside them woods. Plenty o' Rebs walkin' back and to 'long the road, but they ain't seen us. Pretty soon we come up to where we seen the whole camp. Some soldiers was marchin', but I didn't see no guards.

"Look, Lack. See? That the tent where the big army man usta stay. I wish we had me a Reb suit on. Head up close to that tent. Maybe we kin go in it."

Lack stay 'bout a foot back o' me. We sneak real slow, right 'longside the side o' the tent. Wadn't nobody guardin' the door, so I jus' barge right in and run to a cot where some man was 'sleep. "Suh, my name Homer Lusta. I gotta talk to somebody big."

That man come straight up and begin to prattle and blabber. "Who are you? Where did you come from? How did you get in here?"

"We got stuff to tell somebody big. Kin we see the colonel?"

"I am the colonel. Didn't you see the guard?"

"No, suh. We got to tell somebody 'bout them boats."

"Boats? What kind of boats?"

"I don't know what they actual doin'. Curious things is goin' on."

Blest Pete, that colonel begin askin' questions and listenin' while we give answers. He call some other folks in to listen. 'Fore you know it, we done told 'bout everything we knowed 'bout Ed and the captain and Pauline. We told 'em somebody musta kill Charlie and Jim. We told 'em 'bout Gunny.

The colonel told a corporal to go see is that gunnery sergeant come back from 9th Regiment. While he gone, they git us some food from jus' off the food line. We wadn't hardly finish eatin' till here come the corporal and, Blest Pete, Gunny was runnin' in back of 'im.

"Homer! Lack! What you doin' here?" He grab us and pat us on the back.

The colonel final git laxed up. He musta figure they not gonna git 'ttacked by Yankees. We set down for 'bout two hours and them men ask a heap o' questions and we told 'em all 'bout them boat sheds and them station numbers. We answer lotta questions, 'cept we told 'em we ain't got no idea what they got in them boxes. They musta b'lieve what we was sayin' 'cause the colonel told us to rest up and he was gonna send a message to Macon. I 'member Macon.

'Bout noon time, Gunny come back and give us some Reb suits and say we gonna be goin' on a patrol with a big bunch of army boys. Some of 'em goin' to Gainesville and some to Darien and lot more between. Blest Pete, look like we done the right thing. All this stuff goin' on, me and Lack kneel down and give a prayer. I think I hear God answer.

Me and Lack git a long sleep and good chow and we put on them new Reb suits. They give us some new kinda guns. They call 'em rifles and the corporal say they shoot a bullet 'bout half a mile and you don't need no ramrod. Reckon he kiddin'?

The colonel say me and Lack gonna be in the front and guide them boats. We ain't got no skill 'bout guidin' things, but the colonel say don't sweat nuthin' 'cause me and Lack know all 'bout them places we git to go to and we be by his side the whole way. He say be at his tent 06:30 tomorrow.

Next day, me and Lack eat chow and come to the colonel's tent on time. They was Rebs runnin' roun' all over that marchin' field, doin' all kind o' fightin' stuff. Gunny come over to see us and pat us on the back, jus' like last time. "Them things you boys told 'em fit in faultless with stuff the Rebs been hearin' in Macon. They gittin' up a plan to figure out what goin' on and stop it cold."

"Gunny, when is me and Lack gonna actual guide some boats?"

"Can't say. Secret, boys. The colonel gittin' all his plannin' done now, but he say we likely move out soon."

"Is me and Homer gonna be big, Gunny?"

"Big as they come, boys. Big!"

"They ain't mad at me and Homer 'bout leavin' the army?"

"No, Lack. You done what the army say."

Chapter 21

"Battle Cry of Freedom"

@George F. Root

It was December 18. Time been passin' by and me and Lack been workin' harder'n a three-footed rabbit dodging a hungry coyote. The colonel make us practice how to git in and outta them boats real fast and shoot while we doin' it. I hope Carl, over at Station **D**, ain't seen us practicin' in Ed's boat. Ed know we ain't brung it back. I reckon he wonder where we git off to.

Since ain't nobody 'round here 'cept me and Lack never been in them boat sheds, the colonel put us steady workin' with some special men, day after day. We been tellin' 'bout them boat sheds. We showed 'em where them shed bosses hide them telegraph *punchers*. We told 'em 'bout them ladies runnin' the food places. We drawed pitchers on maps showin' wherebout they park boats. We told 'em 'bout the room they got locked up tight so nobody but the boss kin git in. We showed 'em where them people keep guns. We told 'em how to find them channel signs showin' where you come in. We talk a lot and they keep writin' a lot.

Soon after me and Lack git to talkin' with them big people, the colonel git a boat patrol to go hide outside Darien so Grady and Helen's people can't haul no boxes away. He sent 'nuther bunch up to Dahlonega and they sposed to do same thing. They say all the boats gonna be trap up inside. I wish me and Lack could go to Gainesville 'cause that where Ed stay. The colonel say for us not to worry none 'cause we gonna git there.

One thing me and Lack like most was watchin' them boys work that telegraph puncher. I don't understand what they doin', but them people say they kin punch a little handle a few times and Blest Pete, somebody a long way off kin know 'xactly what they was sayin'. They learned us to punch it a few times jus' to see what it feel like. Me and Lack real happy we ain't got to do it 'cause we couldn't make no sense of it.

One failing we told ever'body is nobody don't know what them boxes got in 'em. Seem peculiar. We been haulin' boxes and got no idea what we haulin'. Colonel say if it was dynamite, somebody might set it off at a bad time. Lack say what if guns is in them boxes? That be good for us soldiers, but if they new rifles, we ain't got no new bullets to go with 'em, 'less they mixed 'em in with them rifles.

That poor colonel musta git a big headache with all this. Reckon thass why he the one got a horse, wear pretty suits, got people puttin' up his tent, and gittin' saluted. I told Lack I might would like to be a colonel some day, but I don't think I got sense 'nuff. Lack said he ain't neither, but I reckon he said it 'cause I said it.

One day the colonel git all us together. He git up front and give a speech. "Gentlemen, it's about time. Glad to see Homer and Lack sitting on the front row." He come over and pat both us on the back. "You boys did a good job. No, you did a *great* job, for our beloved South.

"We have a plan and I want everyone to listen and don't miss a thing. For this mission we'll have seven Boat Teams of two boats each: **A, B, D, E, F, G**, and **H**. Each boat will be manned by three well-armed and trained men. Interestingly, each team is named for the shed it will attack. Homer and Lack told us Station **C**, at Bishop, is not used. Our patrols checked that out. Seems it hadn't yet been staffed.

"I ordered a boat patrol of two boats to Darien to stake out station **H** and let no one escape. The other boats of that team will join up in time for the attack.

"I will lead the patrol of two boats in Dahlonega. Gunny, you will command Boat Team **B**. Boat Teams **D, E, F**, and **G** will proceed to their target area so as to arrive, in position to attack, on time. All boats will move out on the schedule I have posted on the wall. I mentioned that I will lead Boat Team **A** in Dahlonega. Homer and Lack and Gunny will be with Gunny in Boat Team **B** and go to Gainesville. All Boat teams will proceed to their targets so as to arrive, in position to attack on Christmas Eve."

I whisper to Lack the colonel done git real serious now, kinda like Pa used to do. The colonel kep' on talking'. "The timing of this operation is critical. All boats will leave according to schedule, and be in position at 05:30 on December 24. That is an order. It is critical.

"At precisely 06:00 on December 24, all boats will move into their assigned channels. The telegraph technician of each team will immediately disable his assigned telegraph machine. We must do that because if a Boat Team does not succeed, the station boss could send an alert. All these telegraph machines must be disabled at exactly the same time.

"Do not cut the wire. I say again, do not cut the wire. Disconnect the wire. Why? After the attack, we must have a way to communicate.

"At exactly 06:10, all Boat Teams will commence the attack their assigned shed. Capture everyone, if possible. Bind them tightly, including the ladies in the eating places across the street. Do it fast and don't allow anyone to touch anything in the sheds. Do not allow anyone to escape. However, do anything necessary, whatever that may be, to succeed."

"Homer, you think he mean shoot somebody if they git away?"

"You gittin' smart, Lack."

"Once you get all the people tied up or otherwise secure, telegraph technicians will re-connect the telegraph wires and punch in a code to indicate you have succeeded and have everything under control. That will simply be to key the letter 'R' for ready: one short, one long, and one short. Once we receive that code from every station, we'll know we're in full control of all the stations."

"Lack, this jus' like a puzzle."

"With all telegraph machines reconnected, the leader of each team will open some of those boxes Homer and Lack have been hauling and see what is inside. And watch out. If they are booby trapped, it could kill anybody close by. Telegraph technicians, you will key a simple short message sayin what is in the boxes. Then stand by for an order from me.

"Might be a few days until we move out, so during that time no one may leave this base, and we will continue to rehearse. Get some rest and be ready when you get the word. I will leave immediately to monitor the activity in Dahlonega. The boat team has already left to patrol Darien. Major Henry will be in command here. He will order each Boat Team to leave at the proper time. Good luck to all."

Gunny taken me and Lack over to a quiet place. "You see what you boys done? You done the Confederacy a real good turn. Wadn't no way I wudda ever thought you boys had it in you."

"Gunny, do we git time to go down to Dodgetown and see Pa and Lotta 'fore we go?"

"No, Homer. The colonel say ain't nobody kin leave till we finish. We gotta stay right here, case things change. This be over soon and I betcha the colonel gonna give you some days off then."

"I reckon Pa wonder what we up to."

"He'll know one day. Right now them boat teams practicin' how to git in and git out. The major want you boys to help 'em learn more 'bout them sheds and that gonna be up to you boys to do."

"What we do?"

"You gonna be big people. You gonna be a teacher and train all us 'bout the sheds. You kin be the diff'rence 'tween winnin' and losin'. Let's go to the practice field and git started."

Me and Lack work hard, hour followin' hour, trainin' big people. They gittin' real good. Gunny come by a few times and say them boys was lookin' good too.

Ever' once in a while the major come over and told 'nuther Boat Team it was time to go and for me and Lack to talk to 'em and answer some more questions they git. Then one day the major told us we got to go too. Lack say if we leave now, itta take 'tween two and three days since we git three in a boat and all us kin paddle and we don't take much rest. Gunny said we need to git there soon 'nuff to git a breather 'fore we attack.

It git kinda scary when we git our food bags, git in the boats, and git on the river headin' north. We spread out and wadn't but two in any boat sposed to show hisself. The other man sposed to lay down and make like he ain't here. We was in Ed's boat and I was glad when we git on up north case Ed seen us. I look up the river and seen that water comin' at me. 'Bout two days from now, we gonna look up and see the big white square channel marker with a **B** on it, ten foot up on a big oak tree. I 'member our trainin' say we ain't gonna jus' blunder in. We sposed to sneak in like a mama cat goin' after a tricky rat.

One thing I hate, is when we git a bad winter rain like the one we got goin' on right now. Ain't freezing yet, but I betcha it will tonight. Glad the colonel give us some overcoats. Maybe if it keep rainin', we kin hit 'em better, 'cause them people in the shed gonna be tryin' to git dry and warm.

We keep goin'. Ain't long now. I hope Ed ain't gonna git mad when he see us. I don't want nobody mad at me. God say not to git mad at nobody. Ma usta say that too. Me and Lack both git more scared every paddleful.

Gunny lean over and told us today is December 24. I say I know. He said how far we got. Lack tell 'im we gonna hit that big oak tree 'bout 03:00. Thatta be good 'cause icy and wet as things is, maybe them men work in the shed gonna be inside, clamorin' for warm things to wrap up in.

I reckon we wadn't goin' fast as we shouldda 'cause when we seen tht big white sign up in that tree with a **B** on it, Charlie's watch say it was 04:45. That kinda good 'cause the colonel say 05:30 was the deadline. Colonel won't know it 'cause our telegraph man ain't gonna turn it off for a while.

"Homer, a **B** on the tree. I reckon we better lay off goin' in the channel, right?"

"Yep, Gunny. See over there 'cross the river. A cove. Both us boats kin git in and wait."

That what we done. And we wadn't too far 'way 'cause we seen ever'thing over there. It seem a long time, but we taken turn dozin' off. I cudn't doze none 'cause I never could when I was 'bout to look down the barrel of no gun. And that rain kep' fallin' and makin' more ice on my coat. Gunny say don't shake it off 'cause it make noise fallin' in the boat.

I ain't seen no moon yet. That good 'cause all us boys used to the weather right now and them shed boys ain't. I kep' wonderin' how Pa and Lotta is. I wish I could see 'em, but ain't no tellin' when thatta be.

I laid down and begin thinkin' what 'bout to happen, I figure best thing I need to do now is pray all us Rebs gonna do our South proud. I ain't never thought hard 'bout doin' good things for my land, but I jus' startin' to. *So, God, you know what I wanna say. Me and Lack and all us boys need some help with what 'bout to happen. Only way all us ever gonna git home is do right. Amen.*

"Homer. Git up. Gotta be close to time."

"Yep, Gunny. Eight minutes. We better git up that channel."

We ease our two boats up that channel and stop 'fore goin' under the canvas flap. Lack told the telegraph man where the wire box was. We ain't seen no sign o' people yet. We come to a stop and the telegraph man jump out and run over to the box with a screwdriver. We all got out guns ready. Seem like he wadn't never comin' back. I begin thinkin' 'bout all them boat sheds 'long the river in the same fix right now. Then, here he come back.

"Git it done?"

"Yeh, Gunny. Cudn't find it for a minute. I hope I git the right wires."

"What time it is, Homer?"

"Charlie watch done stopped, Gunny. It say same time as while ago."

"We better ketch up. Boat Team B. Paddle in. Hurry. And all you boys, git them guns ready. Shoot at anybody pointin' a gun at you."

We paddle our boats in and run under the canvas. First thing I hear was Lack yell, "Gunny. Ten of 'em. They all got guns." I seen Ed and the captain. Our captain!

We hear Ed yell, "You boys put your hands up. Now! Drop your guns and walk over here. Now! With your hands up."

Gunny drawed out his pistol and shot the captain and he hit the ground. Then the office door open and this girl with real black hair come runnin' out. I couldn't b'lieve what I seen. I think it was that Pauline. Gunny shoot again. Two times. He yell at us, "Captain's dead. Shoot fast as you can! Git Ed and them boat handlers. Don't shoot that lady."

I seen Lack go down and I run over to him. "Where you hit, boy?"

"My shoulder, Homer. Hurt bad."

Our boys laid down some good fire with them new guns. But Ed shot one of 'em right in the head. Reckon he was dead 'fore he hit the floor.

I raise my gun up and point it at Ed where I figure his heart was and pull the trigger. He fall down hard and probly won't never breathe another pound o' air.

Then somethin' real hot sting hard in my neck. Like fire. I grab where it hurt and look at my hand. It git same red color like when I usta stick pigs on hog-killin' day. Gunny run over and tie a big bandana like them Mexicans use 'round my neck.

I look at Gunny, "How Lack?"

"Better'n you, Homer. Hold this cloth 'round your neck so itta keep the blood inside."

"What happen?"

"Ed dead. Captain dead. Boat handlers dead, too. We jus' got me and the telegraph man and you and Lack left. Telegraph man sendin' a message to the colonel right now."

"You see that lady. Look like Pauline?"

"Yep. Gone, Homer. I don't how she done it. Jus' whiff 'way like a ghost."

Gunny git us in the boat and head for a doctor in Milledgeville. I look at Gunny. "Take care o' Lack. I don't feel good. Be sure Lack git took care of."

Gunny and the telegraph man git to paddlin'. I told Lack thank God we gonna be goin' four mile an hour. He say, "Hang on, big brother. Be there tomorrow this time. The telegraph man sent a message 'bout gittin' a doctor. You hang on, brother. We gonna see Pa and Lotta real soon."

Reckon I went to sleep. I wake up and some soldiers in Milledgeville was puttin' me and Lack in a mule and wagon. We git to the army base and some doctors put poke-root on my neck. Didn't hurt none. They give me some quinine and wrap me up better. They said do it still hurt and I told 'em I wish I could give it to them and let them 'cide.

I sleep a whole day and when I wake up, Gunny say, "Good, you still with us." Reckon that mean I wadn't dead. Gunny say Lack still bad off, but gittin' better.

They put me and Lack back on the wagon and pile lotsa blankets on. Gunny say he gonna git us home to Dodgetown fast but don't wanna hurt us none. Say we got 'bout 70 mile to go and if we don't have no trouble we be there in three or four days. Nice thing for Gunny to do. I be glad to see Pa and Lotta and I bet Old Bean be glad to see both us.

I can't b'lieve 'bout our captain. And Ed. And all them other people. I don't know who is what. Reckon they jus' crooks or traitors.

I keep on wakin' up. And sleepin' again. Sometime the hurt goes 'way. Sometime it come back cruel. Gunny move my blanket 'round so I feel better. Reckon it work this time 'cause my hurtin' gone 'way. I ain't seein' no better. Reckon that medicine harsh on my eyes 'cause ever' time I wake up I can't see good as last time. Gunny kind to me. Like Ma. They oughta raise him to colonel. I gotta tell some big man.

Gunny fix me up again and gimme some more cold soup. "Much 'bliged, Gunny. Tell me what Ed and them put in them boxes."

"I been tryin' to git you sleep, Homer. Now quit talkin'. You got to rest so we kin git you home to see your pa and Lotta. Got some good news, Homer. Colonel sign up Lack in the army. Final, he gonna be a true Reb soldier. Colonel say he done make both y'all a corporal. Y'all both heroes and right soon, both y'all gonna git a medal for bein' so brave."

"Have a p'rade and a shootin' show, too? Maybe Jeannie kin come to it."

"You go back to sleep. In no time a'tall, you be home."

"I be corporal? And git a medal. Kin you thank . . . ?"

"I will, Homer . . . Homer . . . Homer! Hom . . . ."

Epilogue

"The South Shall Rise Up Free"

©John Hill Hewitt

All this time, me and Old Bob still good friends. We been talkin' lotta months now. We sposed to meet 'bout two o'clock today. I'm setting on his back porch, like I always done. 'Cept this gonna be the last time. Make me real sad. After this, I be back up in my Heavenly Home and he gonna git his writin' done like he pledge first time we meet.

Since we been knowin' one 'nuther, we git to be real good friends. I can't wait till that day we meet up yonder, together, where I live, up on that High Plane. It won't never be no hurryin', not never again. Blest Pete, up there we kin talk all we want, any time we want to.

All these days we been talkin', I told 'im ever'thing I knowed 'bout that War. Back when we git started, Old Bob promise he gonna faithful write it all down. I know he done it, 'cause ever' time I say a single word, that boy write it on his paper, jus' like I said it.

Somethin' been knockin' 'round in my head, though, since God taken me Home, is why all them big people on Earth writin' lopsided stuff 'bout the South, sayin' things ain't true. When Old Bob finish, they

159

gonna have to take it all back. Don't, when I git Home, I might go see St. Peter and tell him to be evermore cautious now on 'bout who he let in.

'Xactly two o'clock, right on perfect schedule, Old Bob scamper 'round the corner, jump up on the porch, and set down in his same blue chair, but this time he look 'round in a curious manner. Blest Pete, I done forgit to turn myself visible when I set down. So when I done that, Old Bob heave a cheerful sigh and show his same old smile.

I told Old Bob my memory 'bout to give out 'cause o' all this work. I ask him don't *he* have no questions 'bout them days. I mighta knowed it when he say thass what been hangin' on his mind too. So we sit down and git ourselfs comfortabler. Ever' time he ask somethin', I give a straight answer. Since I stay up on High now, I knowed all the answers and told 'im ever'thin', 'cept some things God don't want folks knowin', them who ain't cross that River yet.

Old Bob say he curious 'bout Dahlonega. How 'bout them boats and them boxes and stuff? I reckon he right. Itsa big 'un. Edward, Ed we call 'im, he come from England. Me and Lack didn't have no idea 'bout it, but Ed always up to no good. He travel all 'round the South, secret lookin' for people to cheat money outta. He musta think the South git in deep trouble and was more nevous 'bout savin' theirselves from the Yankees than they was 'bout savin' their stuff from the Yankees.

Well, old Ed, he git in good with some big Rebel men in Richmond and they give him a job goin' 'round, checkin' on things, ever'where. He went 'round to Reb factories, banks with money in it, and places look like they got 'portant stuff. He begin mostly hangin' 'round a place over in Dahlonega. Ed didn't have no problem gittin' in. Them big men give him a paper say he kin jus' walk up anyplace, show it, and he git to go right in.

Ed, he rose up to be a big man too. Reb people didn't fret none 'bout what Ed doin'. 'Cause he a big man. 'Fore you know, Ed done set up a bad cheat. He git inside the Dahlonega Gold Mint after the Rebs taken it 'way from the Yankees. He knowed ain't gonna be long 'fore the Yankees send soldiers and git it back, so he begin makin' a plan.

Ed git a bunch o' people, like me and Lack, workin' for him. We all think we was workin' for the Rebs. Ed git us takin' boxes up to Dahlonega. Ed git some special men to load 'em with *gold*, put 'em in boats, and send 'em to Station B in Gainesville. Then, people like me and Lack move boxes, few at a time, so all the gold git spread out 'long the Oconee and the Altamaha at them eight stations. That was goin' on 'fore me and Lack git there. Fact is, when me and Lack git there, the Rebs done quit minin' gold. It was jus' settin' there, with that lawbreaker, Ed, in charge.

Plan was, all the gold was sposed to soon git took to the seaport at Darien. Then when Ed tell 'em, some big people from Spain sposed to bring in boats, load 'em up, and head out for Spain, or somewheres, with all the gold.

Jus' happen, thank God, that me and Lack git nervous one day 'bout things goin' on. That when we stop in Milledgeville. We run and told the colonel what we knowed. If we hadn'ta done it, the South woulda been worser shape that it was after the war. Ain't no doubt in my mind, if Ed woulda took all that gold away, the South, 'stead of takin' a hundred years to get back on track, it woulda took maybe three hundred years. It wudn't even be back yet.

Old Bob have a conniption 'bout that gold story. I ain't never saw no eyes big as his. He begin writin' like a woodpecker when he find a tree full o' bugs and want 'em all to hisself 'fore them other bugs know they there.

Old Bob say he wanta hear 'bout when we git home to Dodgetown. Yep, we had us a p'rade. Gunny drive the mule wagon and Lack set 'side of 'im in the shotgun seat. They wrap me up in blankets and white sheets and lay me down in the wagon on a bed o' blankets, with a Dixie bury-flag layin' over me. A big Flag o' Dixie, 'bout eight foot long, was raised straight up side o' where Lack set. 'Leven little Dixie flags was stuck 'round the wagon sideboard. One for ev'ry Reb state with us in the war. The colonel give all them flags to Gunny and he fix it up. Blest Pete, ever' time that wind whip up, it showed a elegant sight.

I seen that p'rade from cross the Jordan River. Wadn't jus' me. Ma was standin' right side o' me and ever' time I look at her I seen tears rollin' down jus' like she usta do when one o' us younguns git somethin' good happen. I seen so many friends. Even Jeannie was there, wearin' a black shawl. People usta say ain't nobody never cry in Heaven, but after this, I knowed better.

Didn't nobody feel like havin' a shootin' show. Ever'body say too much shootin' been goin' on already. Gunny git Pa to come stand side o' this lady holdin' two little boxes. The lady told us she was head o' the

Confederate Honor Roll Ladies. Gunny brung Lack up front. She give a speech 'bout what Lack done. Said he got to be a corporal and give him a medal from the Ninth Georgia Infantry, the Star of Courage. She pin it on him and his eyes light up like a shootin' star in December.

Then Gunny tell Pa to come up and that lady come up and stand next to Pa. She begin speakin' now 'bout what I done. She say I git to be a corporal, too, and she open up a little box and taken out a Southern Cross of Honor. She pin it on Pa and he stand there, slump over, lookin' like he jus' come outta the cotton field. He couldn't say nothing but jus' wipe his eyes. Nothin' never happen like that in my whole days. Me and Ma was still seein' it from cross the River and her hands was still over her mouth and she ain't stop cryin yet. She look at me with them cryin' eyes and say, "Homer, you and Lack done raise up the Lusta name. Bless you."

Next thing, I knowed, God look in my eyes and told me I done finish down on Earth. Me and Old Bob been friends a long time. We stand and shake hands again and both us, same time, hug one 'nuther. I told Old Bob I be lookin' to read that book. He say he gonna make it true, like he promise.

Both us stand back. Sad. Been a long time since I knowed a friend like him. I wave, then turn invisible, and in 'bout a second I done 'cross back over Jordan. I seen Old Bob lookin' hard like he tryin' to still see me. Blest Pete, I know I be seein' him soon, and we kin walk them Streets o' Gold.

###

.